WARRIOR QUEEN OF SIVAGANGA

Shubendra is an avid traveller who explores places that have fallen through the cracks of mainstream history. An expert on the military history of eighteenth- and nineteenth-century India, his primary interest lies in unravelling long-forgotten stories of early modern India through field research and by analyzing old military accounts. *Warrior Queen of Sivaganga* is his second book.

ALSO IN THE SOUTHERN LEGENDS SERIES

Sultan: The Legend of Hyder Ali

WARRIOR QUEEN OF SIVAGANGA

The Legend of Rani Velu Nachiyar

SHUBENDRA

PAN

First published 2023 by Pan
an imprint of Pan Macmillan Publishing India Private Limited
707 Kailash Building
26 K. G. Marg, New Delhi 110001
www.panmacmillan.co.in

Pan Macmillan, The Smithson, 6 Briset Street, Farringdon, London EC1M 5NR
Associated companies throughout the world
www.panmacmillan.com

ISBN 978-93-90742-29-5

1 3 5 7 9 8 6 4 2

Typeset in Adobe Garamond Pro by R. Ajith Kumar, New Delhi
Printed and bound in India by Replika Press Pvt. Ltd.

For Sangeetha

MADRAS
ARCOT
SRIRANGAPATNA
DINDIGUL
SIVAGANGA
RAMANATHAPURAM

KALAYAR KOIL
SIVAGANGA
KOLLANGUDI

Cast of Characters

Ramanathapuram

JOSE DE PRAY, Jesuit priest and princess Velu Nachiyar's teacher

RAGHUNATHA SETHUPATHI, king of Ramanathapuram and Rani Velu Nachiyar's father

MUTHATHAL NACHIYAR, queen of Ramanathapuram and Rani Velu Nachiyar's mother

MUTHURAMALINGA SETHUPATHI, Rani Velu Nachiyar's cousin

MAPPILA THEVAR, Rani Velu Nachiyar's uncle

GOWRI VALLABHA, a Sivaganga zamindar and Rani Velu Nachiyar's distant relative

VENGAN UDAYA THEVAR, Gowri Vallabha Thevar's son

MUTHATHAL, Udaya Thevar's second wife

Sivaganga

RANI VELU NACHIYAR, queen of Sivaganga

MUTHUVADUGANATHA THEVAR, king of Sivaganga and Rani Velu Nachiyar's husband

THANDAVARAYA PILLAI, prime minister of Sivaganga

MUTHU VIJAYA THEVAR, general of Sivaganga

PERIYA MARUTHU PANDIYAR, general of Sivaganga

CHINNA MARUTHU PANDIYAR, general of Sivaganga and Periya Maruthu Pandiyar's younger brother

UDAIYAL, Rani Velu Nachiyar's personal bodyguard

RAMASWAMY, general of Sivaganga

VELLACHI, Rani Velu Nachiyar's daughter

KUYILI, Rani Velu Nachiyar's adopted daughter and leader of the Udaiyal army

VETRIVEL, a *silambam* trainer

Arcot

WALLAJAH, nawab of Arcot

AMEER-UL-UMARA, crown prince of Arcot and Wallajah's son

Mysuru

HYDER ALI, nawab of Mysuru

PURNAIAH, General of Mysuru

SYED KARKI, commander of Dindigul

TIPU, Hyder Ali's son

The English

MAJOR GENERAL SMITH

LIEUTENANT COLONEL BONJOUR

SIR THOMAS RUMBOLD

COLONEL JAMES STUART

The French

GENERAL DUPRÈS

Southern province rulers

GOPALA NAYAKAR, feudal lord of Virupatchi

MALLARI RAYYAN, a loyalist of the English

VEERAPANDIYA KATTABOMMAN, king of Panchalankurichi

Prologue

BY THE EARLY EIGHTEENTH CENTURY, LARGE TRACTS OF LAND in southern India came under the control of the nawabs of Arcot. The nawabs, who started out as governors under the Mughals, took de facto control of the province as Mughal power declined. They were, for all practical purposes, the true overlords of the land.

The kingdom of Arcot was divided into smaller states, which were relatively independent and ruled by local chieftains – *palegars* and *nayakas*. So long as they pledged allegiance to the nawab of Arcot and paid an annual tribute, the chieftains were left alone. The early nawabs continued expanding their kingdoms by subjugating smaller chieftains further south of their borders. They legitimized their conquests by claiming their hereditary right over these newly conquered lands that were originally part of the Mughal empire. They continued this annexation until they reached the southernmost tip of the peninsula, soon becoming the absolute masters of southern India.

As the years went by, the later nawabs grew weaker but clung on to power and the authority of their predecessors in the same manner rather than by force or goodwill. An uneasy peace was maintained between the nawab of Arcot and the local chieftains of his land.

But these were times of rapid change. Small, upstart kingdoms like Mysuru, under ruthless yet charismatic rulers, started expanding aggressively. Leveraging the technology and arms at their disposal owing to the French occupation, some local chieftains quickly challenged the hegemony of Arcot state. Not one to be cowed down easily, the nawab allied himself with the other European power operating in the region – the English.

The English, on their part, though focused on trade, soon started showing a keen interest in aggrandizing lands for their own benefit. They leveraged their alliance with Arcot – under the guise of helping the nawab gain a stronger hold over his kingdom – to gradually annex the lands of the chieftains within the larger state. The nawab, unaware, wholeheartedly supported the English, who were putting down the mutinous palegars with a vengeance.

But there were many kingdoms within Arcot that were either not on good terms with the nawab or simply ignored his authority and had yet to catch the attention of the English. One such kingdom was Sivaganga.

It was the smaller of the two kingdoms that formed the ancient Marava country, the larger kingdom being Ramanathapuram. These two adjoining kingdoms were at the southern fringes of the Arcot state and, ignoring the authority of the nawab of Arcot, effectively functioned as independent dominions. They were, for the most part, oblivious to not only the power struggle between Arcot and Mysuru but even the machinations of the English that had already reached their borders.

1

Summer of 1735, the royal palace of Ramanathapuram

'SHE WILL BE AMONGST THE BEST FRENCH SPEAKERS OF THE land, my lord.'

The confidence in Jose de Pray's voice was in stark contrast to his lean frame. The frailty of his body betrayed the sufferings he had endured during strenuous journeys through hostile territories, but his voice still maintained its gravitas. The arduous passage from Puducherry to Ramanathapuram had soiled his white robe. A man of limited monetary means, de Pray had no choice but to present himself in a rather shabby manner to his potential employer. Nonetheless, his reputation as a Jesuit priest held him in good stead and commanded the attention of Raghunatha Sethupathi, the ruler of Ramanathapuram.

The king of Ramanathapuram echoed de Pray's comments and made his intentions clear. 'I expect no less. The princess of Ramanathapuram, the scion of the Sethupathi clan, my daughter Velu Nachiyar will grow to become the best French speaker in the land. Under your tutelage, my Velu should have a firm command over the language. After all, she will have to someday negotiate with the French on trade and commerce.'

Jose de Pray's eyes glistened in agreement. 'And she will be, my lord. The princess, with her exceptional linguistic skills, will surprise even the French in Puducherry.'

Satisfied with de Pray's conviction, Raghunatha Sethupathi declared, 'Good! I hereby appoint you tutor to my daughter. You may begin teaching her on a day recommended by our astrologers. The treasury will pay your wages. You will also be given your own personal lodging in the palace until my daughter's education is complete. You may leave now.'

Thanking the king, Jose de Pray walked out of the durbar of the Ramanathapuram palace. He was the last person to have been granted audience with the king that evening. As he stepped out onto the open courtyard, de Pray witnessed the native soldiers practise a drill of the ancient martial art known as silambam. As the soldiers swung long bamboo sticks in a coordinated manner, he watched them, fascinated, having set his eyes on the technique for the first time.

Soon, a courtier came by to escort the priest to his new quarters.

Meanwhile, in the durbar, Raghunatha Sethupathi had barely resumed his position on the throne when another courtier entered.

'My lord, the queen requests your presence. She is waiting for you in her quarters.'

Raghunatha Sethupathi was not a man to keep his beloved wife waiting.

Muthathal Nachiyar was finishing up her letters when a young female courtier ushered the king inside. Turning towards him, the queen of Ramanathapuram began, 'I hear you have appointed a Frenchman to tutor Velu.'

'Yes, dear. One of the very best.'

Muthathal Nachiyar rose from her chair. Even though she was of average height, she looked slight compared to her tall husband. Her neck was bedecked with many necklaces that rested on her bosom, but it was her nose ring that would catch anyone's attention. For her small, stubby nose, it was disproportionately large.

'I understand teaching her the arts of combat and warfare is necessary, as she is the daughter of a warrior. I am also proud that she is learning to wield our traditional weapons – the *valari* and silambam sticks. I beam with pride when I see her riding horses. She is, after all, a daughter of the Sethupathi clan. I am all for this education being imparted to her by pundits far and wide. I fully concur with you that she must learn the language of the Muslims up north. But pray, why are you bringing in the English and the French to teach her those traders' languages?'

Raghunatha Sethupathi replied with a smile, 'The English and the French are more than traders, dear. They have powerful armies and the best weaponry. I haven't seen anyone overcome their advanced battle tactics. Both have brokered power with the Mughals and the Marathas and seem to have limitless resources. They are now trying to forge an empire of their own and so will play a key role in the future of these lands. I don't want our Velu to be caught unaware by the machinations of these people. By helping her learn their languages, we will be doing her a most important favour.'

Muthathal Nachiyar sighed. 'But she is just five years old.'

'She is far more capable than any child her age. Velu will do just fine. Moreover, this is crucial, given our changing times. It is our responsibility to equip her for the uncertain future that lies ahead.'

Harvest season of 1746, the prince's quarters inside the Sivaganga palace

An animated discussion was underway in the prince's quarters. A few men were seated on chairs and a few were standing. One young man, wearing a green dhoti held by a gold buckle, addressed the tall, muscular man in the centre of the room.

'I have heard that she has defeated many a man in sword fights.'

Muthuvaduganatha Thevar, dressed in a fine white dhoti, placed a hand on the scabbard that hung from his hip after hearing his advisor speak. A tinge of insecurity streaked his brown eyes. The young advisor, now wary of dissuading the prince from the proposed matrimonial alliance, quickly added, 'But she is not capable of challenging you, my lord.'

A warm smile crept under Muthuvaduganatha Thevar's trimmed moustache as he spoke, 'My intention is not to challenge her. A martially skilled woman would be a great asset to our kingdom.'

Another advisor chimed in, 'I have heard that she has been given complete independence to lead the cavalry of Ramanathapuram and is effectively their real general. She takes orders from none and spends more time on the field than in the ladies' quarters. We need a princess who enhances the beauty of the court of Sivaganga and not a soldier.'

Muthuvaduganatha Thevar didn't waver. 'Well, a competent general like her would be a welcome addition to our army. As for her beauty, I have no qualms – I have seen paintings of her made by the Ramanathapuram court artists – she will undoubtedly enhance the stature of our court.'

The courtier continued, 'But, my lord, our agents have informed us that she plays an active role in the day-to-day administration of Ramanathapuram as well. The sixteen-year-old princess has the ear of the king. She could potentially be a threat to you when you take over the reins of Sivaganga from your father. She could very well seek to play an active role in the running of our kingdom if we proceed with this alliance.'

'I want someone as proficient as her to help me run Sivaganga,' Muthuvaduganatha Thevar retorted. 'Her support could be valuable. I don't see her as a threat, rather an able administrative advisor. I would like to hear the opinion of our prime minister, Thandavaraya Pillai.'

Muthuvaduganatha Thevar addressed the oldest member in the room – a bald man who had covered his head with a simple white cotton turban. He sat amidst the nobility of Sivaganga, with no ornaments adorning his head gear or neck. Dressed in plain white cotton, he was just a little over fifty years old, but his wrinkled face and the saggy skin around his arms made him look much older.

After listening silently for a long time, Thandavaraya Pillai cleared his throat. He picked up the silver goblet next to him and sipped some water. The strain of being the chief advisor of Sivaganga had clobbered his spirits. Handling the vagaries of Sivaganga's neighbours through tact and diplomacy was a difficult task.

'My lord, I see your heart is set on Princess Velu Nachiyar. I haven't come across a braver or more intelligent woman than her. She is the perfect match for you and will be a great queen for Sivaganga. A matrimonial alliance between you and the princess would strengthen the bond between the two Marava countries – Sivaganga and Ramanathapuram. With the Thanjavur Marathas and the Nawab of Arcot to our north, a stronger Marava is the need of the hour to maintain our independence against our larger neighbours.'

Muthuvaduganatha Thevar climbed the raised platform at one end of the room and announced, 'I would like our prime minister to convey my acquiescence to a matrimonial alliance with the princess of Ramanathapuram to my father, Muthu Vijaya Thevar, the king of Sivaganga. Proceed with the preparations to make a formal request to the king of Ramanathapuram for the hand of Princess Velu Nachiyar.'

Harvest season of 1746, the royal palace of Ramanathapuram

Raghunatha Sethupathi, Muthathal Nachiyar and Velu Nachiyar were all present in the queen's quarters. There were smiles all around.

Muthathal Nachiyar declared with a sigh of relief, 'The matrimonial proposal from Sivaganga finally arrived today. I was a little worried that they were not interested. We should send across our formal acceptance to Sivaganga at the earliest and also begin preparations for the wedding.'

Raghunatha Sethupathi looked at his daughter warmly and asked, 'What do you think, Velu? Are you happy with the marriage proposal?'

'I have only heard great things about the prince, Appa—'

Muthathal Nachiyar interrupted her daughter, 'Of course, you have heard only great things about him. The prince is extremely skilled in the arts of warfare and administration and places religion above all else. He will turn out to be a very competent king. Sivaganga will flourish under his rule.'

Still looking at his daughter, Raghunatha Sethupathi continued, 'Even so, I would like to hear Velu's opinion.'

With a shy smile and her head still bowed down, Princess Velu Nachiyar replied, 'Your decision is my decision.'

Muthuvaduganatha Thevar married Velu Nachiyar with great pomp and grandeur. As time went by, and with the passing of his father, Muthuvaduganatha Thevar went on to become the king and Princess Velu Nachiyar, the queen of Sivaganga.

The summer of 1756, Sivaganga

Rani Velu Nachiyar was alone in her quarters, sitting near her desk with her back to the door, when Muthuvaduganatha Thevar entered the room. The queen quickly wiped away her tears and turned around to greet him.

'Welcome, my dear.'

Muthuvaduganatha Thevar wordlessly came forward and embraced his wife. It was a sight he had grown used to in the last ten years – his beautiful wife sitting crestfallen.

'I am well aware of the things those maids speak behind your back. Don't fret about it. They will not go unpunished this time.'

A smiling rani reassured the king, 'I don't want you to punish anyone. I don't mind their barbs, my love. After all, there is truth in their gossip. I am a barren woman,' she said through a muffled sob.

'No, you are not! And I don't want you to believe that, Velu.' Raja Muthuvaduganatha held the queen closer to his chest.

'It's not about what I believe. It has been nearly ten years and I still haven't borne you a child.'

'It doesn't matter, my love. You have been my partner, my confidante and my source of strength. What more can I ask from you? You're already a good mother to my children – my subjects, the citizens of Sivaganga. While I remained focused on military and foreign affairs, you took over the administration of the kingdom and led us ably throughout these ten years.'

Holding the queen's hands, he led her to the large window overlooking the courtyard in the palace.

'Look outside, Velu. You have streamlined the revenue sources of the kingdom, you have found efficient ways to remove red tape and increase the inflow to the treasury to an unprecedented level. You even helped us reform the tax structure that brought succour to the businesses of the land. There is lasting peace and material wealth in our lands today. There is nothing but praise on the lips and love in the hearts of the citizens for the administration of Sivaganga. Your efforts for the enhancement of our kingdom are nothing short of a mother's love and concern for her children.'

'Thank you, my love,' Velu Nachiyar said with a smile to conceal the doubts that clouded her mind.

I have only one wish, a progeny for you, my love. The day I bear a child for you is the day my life will be complete. For everything that you have given me, a child is the most precious thing I can give you, much more than all the material wealth that you give me credit for.

'Who are those children?' Muthuvaduganatha Thevar suddenly asked, peering down the window.

A young girl and two teenaged boys were standing at the edge of the courtyard and watching the flawless movements of the silambam trainers in awe.

The king called on a maid and demanded, 'Find out whose children they are and get them up here.'

'As you command, my lord.'

Soon, the three children were brought up to the queen's quarters. There was amazement on their faces as they looked around the richly decorated room of the queen. They felt quite out of place in their rustic clothes.

Muthuvaduganatha Thevar addressed them gently, 'I haven't seen you children here before. What are your names?'

If the children felt nervous, they hid it well and responded to the king's question in energetic voices. The taller boy replied first: 'Periya Maruthu Pandiyar'. The other teenage boy said, 'Chinna Maruthu Pandiyar'. The ebullient little girl said her name was Udaiyal.

Curious to know more, Raja Muthuvaduganatha asked, 'Who brought you here?'

'Prime Minister Thandavaraya Pillai brought us as help for the royal household, my lord,' Periya Maruthu Pandiyar responded with even more fervour.

The king was amused and surprised in equal measure. He was sure the children would prove to be good additions to the royal household. He looked up at Rani Velu Nachiyar to find that she was watching the children with great delight and fondness, particularly Udaiyal, the bubbly little girl. This instantly gave him an idea.

There is a lot of energy in these children. The girl would be good company for my Velu. Her presence could drive away Velu's melancholic thoughts.

Acting on his judgement, he announced, 'Udaiyal, you will be part of the queen's personal staff. You boys wait outside for the prime minister to assign you your jobs.'

The two boys exclaimed in unison, 'Yes, my lord.'

Soon, the boys left the room followed by a much-relieved, smiling Muthuvaduganatha Thevar. Little Udaiyal looked up at the queen, wide-eyed. To her, Rani Velu Nachiyar looked like a goddess in her rich and elegant attire. Udaiyal's innocent face made Velu Nachiyar smile tenderly. *Another act of kindness by the king*, she thought to herself.

She bent down and stroked the youngling's silky black hair. 'Welcome to your new home, Udaiyal.'

The winter of 1761, Sivaganga

Udaiyal, now well into her teens, was leaning against a wooden pillar in the corridor of the palace, watching the soldiers training with *marus* and *kathis* in the large, open courtyard of the palace. Even after five years in this place, she was so enamoured by the deft movements of the soldiers that she would grow oblivious of her surroundings. She didn't realize when the queen of Sivaganga came up and joined her in watching the training.

'Impressive!'

Rani Velu Nachiyar's voice pulled Udaiyal out of her daze. Moving away from the pillar, Udaiyal bowed her head to the queen, 'I am sorry, my queen. I didn't realize you were here.'

'There is nothing to be sorry about, Udaiyal. The ancient martial arts of our land are truly a sight to behold.'

'I never witnessed such synchronized movements before coming to Sivaganga, my queen. The sound of the kathis clashing sets my heart racing. The energy in the courtyard leaves me spellbound. I am transported to a different world altogether.'

Looking at the soldiers again, Udaiyal's excitement quickly gave way to disappointment.

The rani couldn't help but notice this shift in her eyes. Placing a hand on Udaiyal's shoulder, she asked, 'Why the sad face, my child?'

'It's nothing, my queen,' the girl lied.

'I am like your mother, Udaiyal. I know when I see sadness on my daughter's face.'

Udaiyal looked up at her mother figure and quietly replied,

'From the day I entered Sivaganga, I have been captivated by the martial arts display here in the courtyard. It has long been my desire to learn these warfare techniques. But I understand I have important responsibilities in the royal household and that I will never be able to learn these arts.'

With her hands still on Udaiyal's shoulders, Velu Nachiyar looked up at the ongoing drill in front of her. How could she not have noticed the young girl's suppressed aspirations?

'I am in need of some bodyguards,' the queen finally spoke, a plan taking shape in her mind. 'I am specifically looking for female bodyguards who can freely move in and out of the ladies' quarters. It will have to be someone trustworthy. Would you like to be my bodyguard, Udaiyal?'

'My life is pledged to your safety, my queen. It will be an honour to serve as your bodyguard,' Udaiyal said earnestly.

'But my bodyguards need to be skilled in our martial arts. They need to be trained like the best of our soldiers.'

With disappointment clouding her face, Udaiyal replied, 'But I have no such training, my queen.'

'Well then, I would like you to be trained in the arts of silambam as soon as you can. You should learn to wield the maru, kathi and *kattari*. It's time for us womenfolk to be as well versed as our men in martial arts. I want only the best of bodyguards around me,' Rani Velu Nachiyar said with a firm but genteel smile.

Udaiyal looked up with glee. But a thought soon washed it away. 'What about my existing responsibilities, my queen?'

'I am confident you can do both and come out with flying colours,' the queen said, caressing her face.

Unable to contain her joy, the young girl fell at the rani's feet.

'Thank you, my queen! Thank you! I will always be indebted to you!'

Helping Udaiyal rise to her feet, Rani Velu Nachiyar replied, 'This is the least a mother can do for her daughter.'

The monsoon of 1766, Sivaganga

Excitement was palpable in every corner of the Sivaganga fort. The soldiers outside the palace gates were dancing and singing buoyantly as the musicians played barrel-shaped percussion instruments known as *thavils*. Traders from the market across the palace had also joined the festivities. Inside the palace, young female courtiers were running in and out of the ladies' quarters with sweets and flowers. The cooks were busy preparing a lavish feast. Astrologers were diligently writing out new charts. High-ranking nobles were congratulating each other. The king of Sivaganga had a wide grin on his face as he proceeded to the ladies' quarters with his entourage.

An old lady walked out of the innermost chamber of the women's quarters. A young girl handed her a white cotton cloth to wipe her hands with. As the old lady looked up and saw the king and his entourage approach, she bowed and said, 'You have been blessed with a beautiful daughter, my lord. We have a little princess in our household. The baby is healthy and doing well. And she bears your resemblance, my lord.'

Beaming with joy, Muthuvaduganatha Thevar took the biggest ring off his right thumb and placed it in the old woman's hand.

'How is my Velu doing?' he asked.

'She is doing fine, my lord. I have seen very few women bear labour pains as well as our queen.'

Muthuvaduganatha Thevar's eyes welled up. He quickly blinked away the tears.

My Velu has suffered the pain of childlessness for twenty years. She has endured barbs and snide remarks with unparalleled dignity. I am not surprised that she bore the pain of childbirth with such fortitude. She is a strong woman. I am thankful that the sadness that had engulfed her for the last two decades has finally come to an end with the birth of our daughter.

Composing himself, the king declared, 'Before I see my wife, I would like to make an announcement to bestow generous gifts to the citizenry of Sivangaga. I want to share my joy with them. Call on my courtiers.'

Before Muthuvaduganatha Thevar could instruct his courtiers to distribute monetary presents to his subjects, a female courtier came rushing towards the king and interjected, 'Apologies, my lord, but the ambassadors from Arcot have arrived and are urgently requesting an audience with you.'

All signs of joy vanished from Muthuvaduganatha Thevar's face upon hearing this unexpected news.

Any news from Arcot is bad news. Our northern neighbours have never wished us well. I better deal with them at the earliest. I will need the best counsel to tackle this matter.

He steadied himself and ordered the courtier in a firm voice, 'Inform the ambassadors that they will be granted audience at the earliest. Accord them all our hospitality as they must be tired from the journey. And bestow them with gifts on the occasion of the birth of my daughter.'

Muthuvaduganatha Thevar called on another courtier, 'Summon the prime minister to my personal quarters tonight.'

The courtier immediately went out to deliver the message. Muthuvaduganatha Thevar recomposed himself and entered the ladies' quarters to share the joy of their newborn daughter with his wife.

Inside the chamber, Rani Velu Nachiyar was lying on the bed with relief writ large on her face. The queen's bodyguard and her most loyal aide, Udaiyal, held the baby in her arms and cooed at her. The king quietly went over to the side of the bed and stood next to his exhausted wife. The rani nodded at Udaiyal who, understanding the queen's command, placed the baby next to her bed and left the room.

Muthuvaduganatha Thevar gently held his wife's hand and looked at their progeny with great pride and warmth. 'Our little one, Vellachi.'

Later that night, when things had quietened down, Thandavaraya Pillai arrived at the king's personal quarters. There were no courtiers present – it was a confidential meeting between the two.

The prime minister began, 'Many congratulations on the birth of our little princess, my lord. I wish the arrival of the ambassadors of Nawab Muhammad Ali Khan Wallajah had been better timed. However, now we need a plan of action to deal with Arcot.'

'Yes, Appa. I'm well aware they are here to demand the annual tribute. They still think Sivaganga owes feudal allegiance to the Arcot empire. They offer us no protection, nor do they help us in any regard. We have been independent since the time of my father. I will not be intimidated by them. We need to put an end to their demands. It's high time they recognize us as an independent kingdom, even if that calls for using force to convey our message.'

Thandavaraya Pillai responded in a calm demeanour: 'The Marava kingdoms of Ramanathapuram and Sivaganga have historically been feudatories of Arcot. The Arcot nawabs have drawn these hereditary rights from the Mughals themselves. But it was through the sheer military force of Wallajah's ancestors that Arcot imposed their will on the Marava countries. Now that Wallajah no longer has his military might, he doesn't have the strength to subdue us. We do not owe him any tribute, my lord.'

'So are you recommending that we go to war with them?'

'No, my lord. Even though the Sivaganga armies are stronger than ever and the Wallajah army is nowhere near its prime, they are much larger. A war will most likely lead them to our lands, and a protracted battle will have a detrimental effect on the coffers of Sivaganga. We need to be wary of the Thanjavur Marathas and Pudukkotai Tondaimans as well. They will not pass up an opportunity to attack us while we're in the midst of a war with Wallajah. All we should do right now is not pay the tribute.'

'Then how do we deal with the ambassadors? I haven't replied to Wallajah's letters for many years. The ambassadors are bound to demand the tribute. If we refuse to pay, Wallajah will construe our rebuff as an act of war!'

'My lord, we need to be tactful with the ambassadors. When they demand the tribute, we will not deny them payment outright. We can simply convey to them that we will pay the monies owed to them in the near future.'

'And when will that be, Appa?'

'Never.'

'Wouldn't that antagonize them?'

'It very well could, my lord. But they will not be able to do anything; they'll have to take our word for it.'

The king looked confused. 'Why do you think so, Appa?'

'Sivaganga is at the southern end of Arcot. Wallajah has bigger problems with his more powerful neighbours further north. The Nizam, the Marathas and the Mysuru rulers are giving him many a sleepless night. If he's smart, he won't risk moving his troops down south, as it will expose him in the north.'

The king was still not convinced by the prime minister's argument.

'So, we are essentially gambling that Wallajah won't attack us because of the present geopolitical tensions. But ego overcomes all rationality, Appa. A man would risk a war and lose it all just to satisfy his pride. I think we are taking a big risk herein, hoping that Wallajah won't attack us. Aren't we pledging the security of Sivaganga on a mere hope?'

'Well, we could look at it as a calculated risk. We are practising statecraft here, my lord. Wallajah is an intelligent man. We will antagonize him for sure. But he will wait for the right opportunity to attack us. I believe now is not the most propitious time for that. But if he does, we will give him a bloody nose. He has more to lose in a protracted war than we do.'

'But this way, we will forever have to live in fear of an attack by Arcot! That's not a future I have envisaged for Sivaganga.'

'We will have to go to war with Arcot at some point to cement our independence, my lord. Let's make that war happen at a place and time of our choosing. By then, we will need to strengthen our borders and boost the numbers in our army. We need to have our treasuries and granaries brimming to sustain ourselves during the war. We have a lot of work to do to secure our kingdom. But eventually, we will be ready. Let us buy ourselves some time by merely offering to pay the tribute and nothing more.'

'Appa, I always trust your advice, and so we will act on your suggestion. Now, what do we convey to the ambassadors?'

'Let us meet them tomorrow itself. We will not question their right to a tribute. We will only convey our inability to pay it right now. Let us tell them our revenue collection has been poor after this year's harvest. We will make a vague promise to pay the tribute in the near future and proceed to shower them with gifts on account of the princess's birth. That should buy us some time.'

2

Post-harvest of 1772, the Sivaganga palace

PERIYA MARUTHU PANDIYAR WAS A GIANT OF A MAN WHO could put a wrestler to shame. His thick moustache, twirled up over his rarely smiling mouth, lent him a menacing look. His signature red vest over a white dhoti further accentuated his intimidating appearance. As did the unusually large sheathed sword that he always carried in his left hand. He was standing next to his younger brother Chinna Maruthu Pandiyar who, in contrast to his name, stood a good couple of inches taller than his elder brother and flaunted a body that was more toned than his periya's. His moustache was twirled up just like his brother's, but it rested on an easy smile. Dressed in all white, with an intricately carved scabbard tied to the left of his belt, he looked like a saviour compared to his brother who had the appearance of a vanquisher. The Maruthu Pandiyar brothers were now standing guard outside the king's personal quarters.

Chinna Maruthu Pandiyar broke the silence. 'I feel concerned every time the king holds private conversations with our prime minister. There is always some trouble round the corner. I want to know what bothers our leaders and how to be of assistance to them.'

His brother growled, 'Chinna Pandi, I care only for the safety of my king. My sword will give a befitting reply to any trouble that comes his way.'

'I don't doubt that, Peri Pandi. I just want us to be part of the conversation.'

Before Periya Maruthu Pandiyar could reply, Thandavaraya Pillai opened the door and said, 'The king wants to meet both of you. Please come in.'

Inside, Raja Muthuvaduganatha was sitting with a hand over his furrowed brow. While his physique didn't give his escalating age away, his hair had turned grey and his moustache white. At the sight of the two brothers, a sense of calm washed over him.

'Peri Pandi and Chinna Pandi, my most loyal generals, come over! There, I can see the frustration in your eyes. Forgive me for keeping you out of our earlier conversation, but I had to have a discussion with someone cool-headed. Hence, I chose to speak with Appa alone,' the king pronounced calmly.

The Maruthu brothers looked at their king in confusion.

Periya Maruthu Pandiyar spoke in an uncharacteristically soft voice, 'You misconstrue our zeal, my lord. We are not as reckless as you think.'

'No, Peri Pandi, and I will prove it you in a moment.'

With the Maruthu brothers still bewildered, the king of Sivaganga continued somberly, 'Our spies in Arcot have informed us that Wallajah is preparing to send an army towards Sivaganga.'

Periya Maruthu Pandiyar immediately drew out his sword

from its scabbard and roared, 'My sword is thirsting for the blood of those dogs! My lord, I would like nothing more than the honour of personally leading our army to vanquish them!'

Chinna Maruthu Pandiyar too raised his sword. 'We only await your orders, my lord!'

'Calm down, you two! See why I didn't involve you both in our earlier discussion? We are not starting a war with anybody. Put your swords back!' the king commanded.

The Maruthu brothers reluctantly slotted back their swords into their scabbards. Once calm returned to the room again, the raja continued, 'We will initiate some backdoor diplomacy to dissuade Wallajah. But, in the meantime, we need to safeguard ourselves as well. I need you both to strengthen the defences of the kingdom. Call in the reserve troops to the barracks and prepare them for battle. Ensure that we have ample supplies and enough arms and ammunition for a long war. Keep our supply chain in order.'

The brothers nodded, but Chinna Maruthu Pandiyar wasn't convinced. 'If we are pursuing diplomacy, then why are we actively preparing for war, my lord?'

'Good! You are thinking! Things are different now, Chinna Pandi.'

Muthuvaduganatha Thevar looked at his prime minister to fill in the Maruthu brothers on the details.

'Arcot has a new ally – the English,' Thandavaraya Pillai began. 'Now, the English are more nefarious than Wallajah. Even a frivolous reason is enough for them to attack and annex neutral territories. They have found the perfect partner in Wallajah, or rather his son, Ameer-ul-Umara, who wants to prove himself a worthy successor. Waging a successful war campaign is a surefire way of earning his stripes as a general of Arcot and the rightful heir to the throne. Meanwhile, Wallajah is still upset that we haven't paid the tributes due to him. He wants to wage a war against us but doesn't want to risk his troops. The English, on the other hand, want to annex more and more lands to improve their revenue. So, they are bringing in troops to do the bidding of the Arcot prince. It looks like all their goals converge if they decide to attack Sivaganga.'

Periya Maruthu Pandiyar interjected, 'It doesn't matter if it's Arcot or the English. We will slay our enemies. We are ready for a war! Diplomacy is not the answer here.'

Muthuvaduganatha Thevar tried to reason with his generals again. 'Peri Pandi, I know we are more than capable of facing our enemies. But the English are a different breed. They don't follow the traditional rules of engagement of our lands. We still don't know the true intentions of Ameer-ul-Umara. It is critical to take the path of least destruction. I don't want to burden Sivaganga with the vagaries of war. We must follow a course that best safeguards the interests of our kingdom. So, we have decided to pay Wallajah a part of the tribute to cool his temper. Some of our diplomats will visit Arcot to offer a multitude of gifts personally to Ameer-ul-Umara and dissuade him from mounting any expedition against us. We will also try and make the nawab, his son and the nobles of the Arcot court see reason in our ways and join us in discouraging the English from taking any aggressive actions. I think this is the best option at our disposal right now.'

A look of disgust spread over the older Maruthu brother's face, which he tried his best to hide.

Diplomacy is for the weak. A fight would solve these problems much quicker.

The younger brother, though, still not swayed by the king's decision, voiced his confusion, 'Why then are we preparing for war?'

The prime minister heaved a sigh and replied, 'We are not sure if Ameer-ul-Umara would listen to his father. Also, Wallajah has very little to lose by sending the English to the borders of Sivaganga. Ameer-ul-Umara may well influence his father to let him and the English attack us. We are more worried about the machinations of the prince of Arcot than his father's. Our stationed diplomats in Arcot have not been able to dissuade Ameer-ul-Umara from talking against us. So, we will have to send out our best diplomats to avert this situation. But if they fail in their mission, we will have to fight a war against Arcot and the English. So we must prepare for any eventuality.'

'When are we sending our diplomats?'

'They are scheduled to leave for Arcot tomorrow itself, with a fifth of the tribute demanded by the nawab and additional gifts to pacify him. They will also carry gold and precious stones to present to Prince Ameer-ul-Umara. That being said, we are not hedging everything on our diplomacy. We need your strength and bravery to overcome any harm that the Arcot prince may bring our way.'

'Our lives have been pledged for the safety and honour of Sivaganga, my lord. We will prepare for war at once.' The Maruthu brothers bowed to the king and took leave.

The next morning, three of Sivaganga's best diplomats assembled in the durbar of Raja Muthuvaduganatha. They were given credentials as representatives of the king. Letters of credit from the bankers amounting to a fifth of the tribute were also handed to them. Everything had been readied to begin the diplomats' long journey towards Arcot. A small armed escort of cavalry and foot soldiers, along with bullock carts carrying gifts for the nawab and his son, were waiting outside the palace gates.

At an auspicious time drafted by the palace astrologers, the diplomats bid farewell to the king and his nobles. Everyone understood the importance of this mission. Failure was not an option. The fate of Sivaganga rested on their silver tongues.

The Maruthu brothers set about readying the army for potential war. Reserves were called in from all villages in the kingdom. Blacksmiths worked in full swing to forge arms for the additional troops. Grain merchants made a beeline for the capital to supply the troops with sufficient grains and other supplies. Thandavaraya Pillai began sending feelers to the local chieftains, seeking support in the event of a war with Arcot. Despite hoping for the best from their diplomats, the Maruthu brothers and the prime minister were preparing for the worst.

Nearly a month after the diplomats had left, a messenger from Arcot arrived at the gates of the Sivaganga palace. He was escorted to the durbar where the king was seated on his throne, anticipating some news.

'I come bearing good tidings, my lord. Nawab Wallajah, cordially welcomed our diplomats and accorded them with the highest distinction. The diplomats won over the nawab and he graciously accepted the payment of our tribute. He declared he wanted to maintain good relations with you, my lord, and expects payment of the remaining tribute as soon as we are in a position to do so. The hospitality extended to our diplomats in Arcot was unmatched. They are scheduled to leave for Sivaganga in a week's time, bearing gifts from the nawab himself.'

Muthuvaduganatha Thevar relaxed a little. 'That is great to hear! We have staved off a potential invasion from Arcot. Our diplomats have done a remarkable job in convincing the nawab with just a fifth of the tribute. How did Prince Ameer-ul-Umara react to our gifts? Were our diplomats able to meet the English representatives?'

'The prince was not in Arcot, my lord. Nor were the English representatives. Unfortunately, our diplomats could not meet them and deliver your gifts.'

The king leaned forward. 'That's strange. Did anyone inform our diplomats about their whereabouts?'

At that very moment, Chinna Maruthu Pandiyar entered the durbar. He came to stand next to the messenger and replied to the king's query.

'I know where they are, my lord. The prince of Arcot and an English detachment led by Major General Smith and Lieutenant Colonel Bonjour have moved south. They were found camping just north of the border between Arcot and Sivaganga. Their intentions are unclear at present, but I think they are gearing up to attack us. We need to pre-empt any action from them. I propose we take the battle to them. The army awaits your orders, my lord.'

'What is this treachery?' Raja Muthuvaduganatha stood up, agitated.

Addressing the messenger, he continued, 'Go back to Arcot immediately and inform our diplomats about the movement of the English troops and the Arcot prince north of our border. We need Wallajah to call back his troops!'

The messenger hastened out of the durbar. A horse was waiting for him to race back to Arcot. The king then declared, 'Bring me Thandavaraya Pillai and Periya Maruthu Pandiyar immediately!'

The courtier ran out with the king's orders. Within a few minutes, the prime minister and the general were in the durbar.

'Ameer-ul-Umara and the English have arrived at our northern borders. This is treachery! That scoundrel Wallajah!' the king exclaimed, getting up from his throne.

Thandavaraya Pillai was stunned into silence for a moment before he could regain his composure and respond to this development. 'We must get our troops to the border as soon as possible. Close the gates of the Sivaganga fort!' the prime minister ordered.

Periya Maruthu Pandiyar's eyes turned red as he clenched his jaw and gripped his sword until his hand turned white. Unable to keep his cool any longer, he growled, 'I will rain death on those dogs! The grounds of Sivaganga will soak in the blood of those mongrels! Order us, my lord! Order us into battle!'

Chinna Maruthu Pandiyar was not far behind. Unsheathing his sword, he cried, 'My sword thirsts for the blood of those English scoundrels! Give us your command, my lord!'

The fervour in his durbar caught up with Muthuvaduganatha Thevar, as he added, 'I will personally lead the assault against

Arcot. Assemble the army now! We will confront them right at the border!'

The generals raised their swords in the air and declared, 'For the King! For Sivaganga!'

Preparations began in earnest to move the army to the border. Thandavaraya Pillai worked with the bankers to procure money and credit to sustain the army. The Maruthu brothers despatched orders to various chieftains throughout the kingdom to send in men and arms; instructed their men to block all approaches to the capital using large trees and dig trenches to slow any troop movement; and directed the construction of military posts in the north of the kingdom for faster communication. The king ordered his scouts general, Ramaswamy, to lead the advance troops to the border and send scouts to locate the Arcot and English camps.

As the scouts and advance troops made their way to the border, Rani Velu Nachiyar got the administration into overdrive to ensure a steady supply-chain. Soon, the entire kingdom was working like a well-oiled, zealous war machine. Everyone confidently believed that Prince Ameer-ul-Umara and the English would be taught a fitting lesson for plotting against and provoking the brave souls of Sivaganga. Raja Muthuvaduganatha and the Maruthu brothers were to personally lead the army of soldiers to the camp set up by the advance troops.

In less than a month, Sivaganga's main army was ready to leave the fort. A day before marching out of Sivaganga to their posts, the king was alone with Rani Velu Nachiyar in their personal quarters.

The queen was dressed in a red saree of the finest Kanchipuram silk with a wide golden border. Her thick, black hair, pulled back and tied elegantly with a gold ornament, now had streaks of white that resembled lightning on a dark night. There was just enough gold on her neck and hands to exude elegance, but all the grace and radiance of her attire couldn't hide the worry that hung heavy on her face.

'Something does not feel right. I insist on coming with you to the army camp. I could support the army as an additional general!'

'You are far more capable than a general, my love. I need your help in more important matters. I need you to stay back to look after the administration of the kingdom and protect the civilians.'

'We will be facing a strong adversary, my lord. I insist that I fight alongside you and actively protect our kingdom. There are capable administrators here to run the kingdom while we defend our borders. I want to be with you as you face our enemies. Please let me come along.'

'But you will be with me in my heart, Velu. I need you to trust my decision. I have no doubt in your ability to vanquish our enemies. However, I cannot risk putting the queen of Sivaganga in mortal danger. For the safety of our kingdom, you must stay back. As your husband, your security is paramount to me. We have a child now, Velu. I could never bear losing you or little Vellachi. Please stay here, safe and secure.'

'I resolutely trust you and your decisions, my lord. But my heart is restless. I want to be by your side.'

'There is no reason to worry, my love. We have competent people in our fold who will help us overcome this crisis.'

'At least take Udaiyal and my other personal guards with you. Trained in the silambam arts just like our men, and thoroughly devoted to the royal household, they have become the best bodyguards in the land. They will stay close to you and protect you.'

'The brave Udaiyal will protect what's most valuable to me – you and our daughter. She will remain in Sivaganga and keep you both safe.'

Before the queen could reply, Raja Muthuvaduganatha stepped forward and wrapped his wife in a tight embrace.

'I will be safe, Velu. Don't you worry.' The queen had no choice but to give in to his request.

The next day, an hour before leaving the palace, the king requested the prime minister's presence in his personal quarters. Thandavaraya Pillai entered to find him waiting in full armour. The raja's eyes welled up with tears, but he didn't feel the need to hide his emotions from the man he considered a father figure.

'Appa, I was just with Velu. She wants to come with me to the battlefield.'

'I wouldn't recommend that, my lord.'

'That's exactly what I said to her. She hasn't taken part in military affairs for a long time now, yet I have no doubt she will be a strength in my arm in battle. But how could I put the most important person to me in a perilous situation? As a husband, how could I put my Velu in harm's way? She just wouldn't listen,' the king said, on the verge of breaking down.

The prime minister put a gentle hand on his shoulder and said, 'It is a tough decision, my lord. But we need an able leader to take care of the kingdom while you are away. There is nobody better than our rani. She has ably led Sivaganga's administration and treasury for years now. Our kingdom will remain safe under her guidance. It is in everyone's best interest if she stays back.'

'Yes, that is true. But she just wouldn't let me go. She kept insisting on being by my side as she sensed danger looming over our kingdom. It was a difficult and emotional conversation, but I finally managed to convince her to stay back for the sake of Vellachi.'

'I fully understand, my lord. However, your decision is correct. I have also asked Udaiyal to stay back here in Sivaganga to protect the queen and the princess.'

Muthuvaduganatha Thevar's mind now turned to more urgent matters. His usual stern expression returned to his face as he wiped away the tears.

'Appa, as you know, we will be camping just beyond Kalayar Koil, close to our borders. That would be our base. It is surrounded by thick forests on three sides, providing us ample protection from our enemies. Our supply lines will be connected to Sivaganga and it would serve as the nerve centre for our operations. I understand your desire to join us too. But given your age and the need to protect my family, I would like you to take Velu, Vellachi and all the ladies of the palace to Kollangudi. I have discussed this with Velu already and we think the palace may not be a safe haven given the circumstances. As you know, our enemies have enough spies and assassins who could harm my family. I can only trust you with this.'

'Yes, my lord. I promise to protect your family with my life; they will be safe with me. I will pray for the success of our troops and wait eagerly for your return with stories of success and valour.'

'Thank you, Appa.' Muthuvaduganatha Thevar's eyes were brimming with gratitude.

'I do have one request, my lord,' Thandavaraya Pillai continued. 'Please attempt to negotiate with the prince of Arcot and the English one last time. I suggest sending them a letter asking for the reason behind their presence at the border. We should exhaust every possible option before we spill the blood of the brave boys of our kingdom.'

The king smiled at his father-figure.

Appa wouldn't give up on a peaceful option even as we are on the brink of war.

'You are right, Appa. I will send messengers to ascertain the reason behind their recent actions. Let us not abandon the path of peaceful resolution until it is inevitable.'

'Thank you, my lord. May the gods shower you with glory in your endeavour!' Overcome with emotion in these dire times, the two embraced, with the hope of emerging victorious on the other side.

The Sivaganga army had a good mix of silambam warriors, men wielding the traditional bamboo sticks, *aruvals* – bill hook machetes, and some, the deadly valaris – medium-sized knives in the shape of a boomerang. Two small cavalry units protected the rear and vanguard of the foot soldiers. A large number of civilian Maravars, farmers, herdsmen and others, who were not soldiers, had also joined the group to fight for their king. They marched forward, wielding small machetes and sharp agricultural tools. The Maruthu brothers and the king led this army to the new base at Kalayar Koil.

The advance troops were setting up camp when the main army crossed into Kalayar Koil and reached the campsite. The newly arrived soldiers quickly unloaded their supplies and began helping the advance troops in setting up camp. By nightfall, the camp was in place and the soldiers lit bonfires after finishing their light dinner. Everyone was chipper and eager to take on their enemies.

The king, along with the Maruthu brothers and his other generals, was putting up in the largest tent in the camp. The good spirits that filled the entire base seemed to emanate from here. A small bonfire was lit right outside the camp, just beyond the entrance. Two soldiers stood guard outside.

Muthuvaduganatha Thevar sat on a round *masand* at one end of the tent while the generals sat in two lines in front of him.

Ramaswamy, the general of the scouts, began speaking, 'Our scouts are scouring in all directions to ascertain the exact location of the English and the prince of Arcot. Once we have identified where they are, we can move our troops and initiate the attack. The element of surprise is bound to bode well for us.'

Chinna Maruthu Pandiyar interjected, 'I am surprised that our scouts still haven't located the enemy camp. They know the terrain of the land. The job should have been done by now. We need to know our enemy's position at the earliest. I have sent some of my men as well to help us locate their camp faster.'

There was a noticeable grimace on Ramaswamy's face.

Raja Muthuvaduganatha didn't want discord amongst his council members even before the start of the battle. Trying to defuse the situation, he responded, 'Yes, Chinna Pandi. Our troops know the terrain well. Now that we have additional men on the lookout for the enemy's position, we should have their exact coordinates by the end of this night. Our enemies are certainly not far. The troops are primed and ready to go. We can begin our movement early tomorrow morning after breakfast.'

Not to be left out from giving inputs in the war council, Periya Maruthu Pandiyar said with a straight face, 'Yes, definitely after breakfast. We need all of our energy to slay those English fools. A nice, heavy and sumptuous breakfast is a must!'

A rare smile lit up Muthuvaduganatha Thevar's face. Nodding in agreement, he said, 'Yes, a good breakfast is much needed. We have a big day tomorrow and everyone needs rest. I want all of you to retire to your tents. We will chalk out the plan of action once we receive news from our scouts.'

The Maruthu brothers and other generals left the tent. The king was now by himself. He didn't plan to retire to his bed yet. Instead, he stood up and walked towards the brown leather-covered wooden box next to his bed. Undoing the leather strap gently, he opened the wooden top. Inside were pagodas – minted gold coins, a dagger and a scroll case. He removed the scroll from its case and touched a finger to the red wax seal of Sivaganga, without breaking it.

Just before leaving the capital, Muthuvaduganatha Thevar had requested his prime minister to draft a letter to Major General Smith, the leader of the English contingent who had camped across the border of Sivaganga. The king had carried the letter discreetly among his valuables.

This letter is the last resort to maintain peace. I pray to the Almighty that I can have this delivered to the English before we draw our swords.

The letter contained details of all the arguments supporting Sivaganga's request for peace. The main point of contention with Arcot was the tribute. The letter stated that a part of the tribute had already been paid with a sovereign promise to pay the rest in due course, thus removing the major cause of disagreement between the two kingdoms. There was no reason for aggression from Arcot now. The letter also broached that Sivaganga never had a history of enmity with the English. So, with the payment of the tribute to Arcot in place, the English had no reason to initiate hostilities in their capacity as an ally of Arcot. He offered to negotiate a settlement. The letter was missing one thing – the location of the addressee. His scouts were yet to return with the English officer's whereabouts.

Once I know his location, the letter can be handed over to him and I can hope for a peaceful resolution. I will not be able to sleep until a scout comes to me with the location of the English leader.

The king placed the scroll back. Still holding the case in his hand, he closed the box and went back to sit on his masand. He would wait for his scouts.

After what seemed like an eternity, the guard soldier entered the tent.

'A scout has come back to the camp and wishes to meet you, my lord,' he reported.

'Send him in,' the king said, quickly standing up.

An exhausted scout staggered into the tent and bowed before him.

'My lord, I have found out the location of the enemy army. They are at two locations.'

'Good! Where have they camped?'

'The bulk of the army is a few hours beyond the forest north of the Shiva temple. The entire Arcot army and the larger English contingent are here. They are camped in a clearing. There is another small group comprised only of English troops. They are further north on the path towards Pudukkottai. This group seems to have a high-ranking English officer in their midst.'

Muthuvaduganatha Thevar's eyes opened wide.

The high-ranking officer must be Major General Smith. He might move south just before the attack. I need to pass on the letter to him before he makes his move and it's too late.

'Good job! Take this letter immediately to the smaller camp. Identify yourself as the messenger of Raja Muthuvaduganatha Thevar of Sivaganga. Deliver this letter to the man who identifies himself as Major General Smith. Hurry now!'

The scout had now turned into a messenger for the king. It was dark outside the tent except for the fading amber lights from the dying bonfires. A couple of soldiers came towards him with water and a packet of food. The messenger gulped down the water and tied the food packet to his waist. He clambered onto a horse that had been readied for him and galloped into the forest.

3

Post-harvest of 1772, the English camp near the Sivaganga border

THE SUN WAS SLOWLY RISING ON THE HORIZON. THE CHIRPING of birds had started transmitting through the air. Major General Smith was sitting with his officers in the dining tent, having his breakfast of unleavened bread and a broth made of boiled meat thickened with peas and flour. The broth was complemented with tea, a luxury afforded only by the officers in the camp. Not a thing seemed out of place in the tent or on the field at Sivaganga's border. Everything was going according to plan.

A few weeks prior to the arrival of the Sivaganga diplomats in Arcot, Wallajah had acceded to Ameer-ul-Umara's persistent request to attack Sivaganga on grounds of Muthuvaduganatha Thevar's failure to pay the tribute despite multiple reminders. Ameer-ul-Umara assuaged his father's fear of the loss of the Arcot troops in this expedition by proposing to take his personal army along with the soldiers of their new allies, the English. The prince also promised to foot the expenses of the English for this expedition with money from his personal treasury. The English, on their part, were more than eager to team up with the prince, as it gave them an opportunity to strengthen their alliance with Arcot, gain a foothold in Sivaganga and, possibly, even favourable trading rights – all at a fraction of the cost that they would have otherwise incurred. With all permissions accorded, Ameer-ul-Umara had begun moving south towards Sivaganga.

Major General Smith, the leader of the English contingent on this expedition, soon slowed down with a faction of his personal soldiers. The bulk of the English troops continued moving with Ameer-ul-Umara's soldiers. Lieutenant Colonel Abraham Bonjour was given the overall command of the English army moving south.

The major general apprised the East India Company council in Madras of the latest developments in Arcot and negotiated with the Tondaiman princes of Pudukkottai for favourable trade terms, as their territory lay on the way to Sivaganga. With all things moving as planned, the major general was able to afford a lazy breakfast that morning.

The serene mood in the dining tent was broken by a native subedar entering the tent.

'Sahib, a messenger from the ruler of Sivaganga has arrived. He bears a letter that he intends to present to you. May I show him inside?'

Major General Smith replied, 'I will meet him in the main tent after I finish my breakfast.'

The messenger was already inside when the major general entered the tent along with his officers. The messenger bowed before them and presented the scroll case.

Unlocking the case, Major General Smith took out the letter. He broke the seal and perused the contents to find that it was not in English. He then passed it on to one of his officers for translation.

Closing his eyes, he patiently listened to the officer.

Once the letter had been read out, the major general ordered his officer, 'Provide some food to the messenger and fodder to his horse. Ask him to stay here until he is told otherwise.'

I need to find a way out of this predicament, and I need to find it fast. I was completely unaware of the tribute paid by Muthuvaduganatha Thevar to Wallajah. This entire expedition is potentially based on a false premise. This matter is bound to be brought up in the council at Madras. All hell will break loose. Our credibility, our ability to negotiate trading rights and our reputation are all at stake here. I don't want to complicate affairs by starting a war. I will need to cease our activities.

He called on his writer. 'Draft a letter to Wallajah asking him to confirm the payment of the tribute. Arrange for a messenger to deliver that letter to the nawab at the earliest. We must also send a message through our scouts to Lieutenant Colonel Bonjour, dissuading him from taking any action until further notice.'

He paused for a moment, then continued, 'I will personally write a letter to the ruler of Sivaganga. We will not pursue any aggressive measures until we receive further information from Arcot. Ask the messenger from Sivaganga to take it back to his king.'

Major General Smith went to his personal tent, which was a much smaller structure with just a bed to sleep in. A teak table and chair that served as his office during war campaigns were the only other pieces of furniture inside the tent. An hour had passed before he came out of his tent, carrying a scroll case. All this while, the Sivaganga messenger had been waiting outside the tent.

Major General Smith handed over the scroll case to him and said, 'This is the reply of the English to your king's plea. Hand over this letter to him.'

Taking the scroll case, the messenger mounted his horse and rushed back to the Sivaganga camp.

Soon after the messenger was out of sight, Major General Smith instructed his officers, 'Break camp. We are heading back to Madras. The governor will decide the next course of action.'

As Lieutenant Colonel Bonjour received and read the letter sent to him by Major General Smith, he grew livid. He rushed to the largest tent in the camp – that belonged to Prince Ameer-ul-Umara.

The prince of Arcot was a young man of medium height. He had a well-trimmed beard, but it didn't hide his boyish looks. A man of rich taste, he wore a richly adorned headgear that matched his intricately designed, cream-coloured kurta. He had lavished himself with the choicest jewellery and the best *attar*. He was clearly not dressed for war. The fragrance of rose filled the tent, which was decorated with thick drapes and floral silk hangings. Despite being pitched so close to hostile territory, the tent's grandeur would have given stiff competition to the durbar of Arcot. The prince was jarred by the sudden entrance of a man dressed in a red-and-white ensemble with a sword dangling around his hip.

'I just received a letter from Major General Smith, your highness. He wants us to hold off the attack,' Lieutenant Colonel Bonjour said with urgency.

Ameer-ul-Umara stood up from his masand. 'What! Why?'

'It seems the king of Sivaganga has already made peace with your father. The major general has asked me not to proceed against Sivaganga.'

The prince felt uneasy. He started rubbing his shaking hands together.

I will be a laughing stock in Arcot. All those plotting against me will use my retreat from this war as an excuse to put me down in front of my father. I will be called a coward!

In a trembling voice, Ameer-ul-Umara began, 'This can't be. I have planned everything to the dot. We can't fall back now! I have staked a lot for this expedition. We can't stop now.'

'I completely agree, your highness. We have a lot to lose if we don't proceed.'

Ameer-ul-Umara was still agitated despite Lieutenant Colonel Bonjour's reassuring words.

I can't go back. My reputation is at stake. This expedition can help me prove to my father and the nobles of the court that I am a worthy successor to the throne of Arcot. I, too, will expand the boundaries of Arcot, like my ancestors did decades ago. Adding more territory under the direct control of Arcot will burnish my position as the true heir to the throne. I will not go back! The die has been cast, and I will go ahead with my plan!

Ameer-ul-Umara regained his composure. He spoke in a firm voice, 'I will not back down. I have invested a lot of my men and money into this expedition. I want the gold at Kalayar Koil, and I will capture the Sivaganga fort. If the English want Sivaganga, they will fight alongside me here. If you want any part of the gold at Kalayar Koil, you will fight alongside me, Bonjour. For if I were to proceed on my own,

Sivaganga will be under my tutelage and the English will not get anything. I will keep the gold for myself, and you will not get a penny!'

A look of concern spread over the English officer's sunburnt face as he thought to himself:

The prince wouldn't stand a chance against the soldiers of Sivaganga. The soldiers of Arcot are not battle-hardened and have the propensity to retreat at the first sign of defeat. I wish I could call the prince's bluff. But I can't risk the legendary gold at the Shiva temple in Kalayar Koil. I need to get my hands on that treasure. I don't care if we, the English, get Sivaganga or not, but I can't lose the gold. I need to play along for now.

'The loyalty of the English towards Arcot is cast in iron, your highness. Neither the English nor I will ever let you down. You have my word, your highness. If you choose to lead us into battle against Sivaganga, it is our duty to follow you and bring you glory,' Bonjour reassured the nawab's son.

Ameer-ul-Umara heaved a sigh and smiled. His eyes gave away his inner thoughts. There wasn't an ounce of doubt in his mind now. He was sold on the word of the English officer.

'I am very happy with your decision, Bonjour. I presume you will deal with Major General Smith?'

'Yes, your highness. My cause is just. I am fighting for the allies of English. I can't let the honour of the English down. I am sure Major General Smith will understand the decision we take here.'

'Good. So, we stick to our original plan?'

A sly smile appeared on Lieutenant Colonel Bonjour's face. He replied, carefully choosing his words, 'We may need to change our plan slightly. Things have become much easier now, your highness.'

A bewildered Ameer-ul-Umara asked, 'What has become easier?'

'The messenger brought more than a letter to me. He also informed me that another messenger had been sent to the king of Sivaganga to convey that there will be no hostile action against him.'

The English officer paused, expecting the prince to understand his devious plan. But Ameer-ul-Umara still looked confused. Bonjour had no choice but to explain his strategy in detail.

'The Sivaganga king will let his guard down, believing every word of the letter sent to him. His troops may even retreat from the border if no attack is expected. We will lure him to the Shiva temple in the forest just outside Kalayar Koil using the turncoat, Ramaswamy. We will set up an ambush there. At an appropriate time, we can take out the king and lay our hands on Kalayar Koil in one fell swoop and even seize Sivaganga itself. Our investment of a few hundred pagodas in Ramaswamy's pockets a few weeks ago should pay us back now!' Bonjour smirked.

Ameer-ul-Umara's eyes opened wide in admiration. He was struck by the genius of the English officer.

'That is a brilliant idea. With you by my side, I can take on any power that rises against us. Liaise with Ramaswamy, pay him more if necessary, and have him bring the king to the temple. Meanwhile, let's move our troops towards Kalayar Koil in preparation for the ambush.'

'Yes, your highness.'

Back at the Sivaganga camp just outside Kalayar Koil, there was a palpable sense of relief on Muthuvaduganatha Thevar's face after reading the letter from Major General Smith. He called in his generals to relate the developments.

'I have received Major General Smith's reply to my letter. He has agreed to cease all combative activity and withdraw his forces from our borders. The major general is now seeking confirmation from Wallajah about the partial payment of the tribute made by us. I am sure the nawab will vouch for our payment. I think we may have successfully averted a war here,' the king's voice boomed.

The Sivaganga generals stood silent. There was no elation amongst them. For they were ready to go to war, eager in their pursuit of glory on the battlefield. This sudden change in their course of action was acknowledged by deflated spirits. But the wisdom of their king would always take precedence over their desire for war.

There was an easy smile on the king's face, who knew all too well the reason behind the thick silence that had descended upon his generals.

I never wanted to risk the lives of my citizens in the pursuit of glory in war. I will take the modesty of peace over it any day. My generals may be disappointed with my decision, but getting all my men safe and sound back to Sivaganga is far more important to me.

'We will break camp and head back to Kalayar Koil. Once the Arcot and English soldiers have withdrawn, we will move back to Sivaganga. Begin preparations by dawn tomorrow. Send out the supplies ahead of the troops. Prepare a grand dinner on account of averting a war today,' the king instructed, his smile intact.

The order was transmitted throughout the campground, and the exercise of closing the camp began in earnest.

Later that night, after the king had finished a rather heavy celebratory meal and was back relaxing in his personal tent, General Ramaswamy sought his audience. In a relaxed tone, he began, 'My lord, it's only through the divine intervention of Shiva that we averted war today.'

'Yes, the gods have been gracious to us today.'

'I believe we must offer our thanks. The Shiva temple just outside Kalayar Koil would be the most apposite for this. We should seek blessings at the temple before leaving for Sivaganga and you should bestow some gifts, too.'

'That's certainly good thinking, Ramaswamy. We should pay our respects to Lord Shiva for today's success. Make arrangements to visit the temple tomorrow morning. I would like to donate generously to the temple.'

'Thank you, my lord. I will arrange for us to leave early in the morning tomorrow.'

A satisfied Ramaswamy exited, bidding his king a good night.

The next morning, as the soldiers began the final process of breaking camp, the king and his personal guards, accompanied by the Maruthu brothers and Ramaswamy, got ready to visit the Shiva temple. Just as they were to mount their horses, Ramaswamy placed another request before the king, 'I think it would be a violation of the sanctity of the temple if we were to enter the premises with our weapons, my lord. We are going to express our gratitude for the peace. Let's leave our swords, valaris and silambam sticks here.'

Chinna Maruthu Pandiyar intervened, 'That's not necessary.

We should not part with our weapons, no matter where we are going. We will ride with our weapons, and we will perform the pooja with our weapons by our side.'

Ramaswamy looked pleadingly at the king, who struck middle ground. 'I need to pay obeisance to the lord. We can carry our weapons right up to the temple, but not inside. My personal guards will hold on to their weapons and stand guard outside. We should not offend the lord this way.'

The king's word was final. So, the personal guards held on to their silambam sticks and valaris, Chinna Maruthu Pandiyar held on to his sword and Periya Maruthu Pandiyar armed himself and got his Mandai war dogs along. The group steadily made their way to the temple.

The Shiva temple was located in a sacred area within a larger complex enclosed by thick walls. Next to the main temple was a *pushkarni*, a water tank. In front was a covered courtyard held up by stone pillars. The entire complex was surrounded by dense forests with only a mud trail leading up to the temple.

The group followed the trail to get to the entrance. As decided earlier, upon reaching, Muthuvaduganatha Thevar removed the belt that held his sword and passed it to Periya Maruthu Pandiyar. In a surprise move, the general unarmed himself and handed both weapons to a personal guard stationed at the entrance.

'I am coming with you inside, my lord. I will not let you go unprotected and alone.'

The younger Maruthu brother was next to hand over his weapons to the guards. 'I am coming in too,' he declared emphatically.

Ramaswamy, who was silently watching the Maruthu brothers, stepped forward and said, 'I will come in as well.' And with that, he handed his sword to the personal guards.

Once the king and his entourage had taken their assigned places inside, the chief priest began chanting the ritual hymns while some others busied themselves with lighting lamps and adorning the idol of the deity with gifts from the king. As the rituals progressed, a few priests went over to ring the giant bells outside the main temple. Almost on cue, muffled sounds were heard from outside.

The Maruthu brothers sensed something wrong. But the noise outside was drowned out by the ringing of the bells. It was only after the Mandai war dogs began barking frantically and the commotion outside grew louder that the Maruthu brothers rushed out of the temple to the source of the chaos. As soon as the generals dashed out, Ramaswamy, who had been standing behind the king all this time, stealthily removed the dagger hidden underneath his clothes. Gripping it tightly, he moved forward to slit the king's throat. Sensing movement behind him, in a split second, the king caught hold of Ramaswamy's wrist and tried to push it away from his neck. On hearing his king's cry for help, Periya Maruthu Pandiyar, who was close on the heels of his brother, turned back towards the temple and witnessed Ramaswamy's attempt on the king's life. Periya Maruthu Pandiyar ran back to the temple and, without wasting a single moment, hit Ramaswamy on the head. The impact was so hard that the perpetrator lost his balance. Raja Muthuvaduganatha released himself from Ramaswamy's grip and pushed him to the ground. The latter dropped his dagger, dazed by the blow. Almost instantly, the loyal general picked up the dagger and slit Ramaswamy's throat.

Chinna Maruthu Pandiyar also came running back, looking panic-stricken, to exclaim, 'The English and Arcot soldiers have ambushed us! Our guards will not be able to hold out against them for long. We need to escape now!'

One look at the withering Ramaswamy lying on the ground, with blood gushing out from his neck, the blood-soaked dagger in Periya Maruthu Pandiyar's hand and Muthuvaduganatha Thevar grabbing onto the side of his neck told Chinna Maruthu Pandiyar everything that had happened. Ignoring the dying man, he said, 'We will scale the walls behind the temple and escape to the main camp.'

The two generals and the king ran to the back of the temple but found the walls too high to scale. Chinna Maruthu Pandiyar knelt down to hoist his elder brother to the top of the wall. The king was hoisted next. Once at the top, Periya Maruthu Pandiyar and Raja Muthuvaduganatha pulled the other general up. A few English sepoys saw the three men coming down the other side of the wall. Fitting their muskets with bayonets, the sepoys charged towards the escapees. No sooner had they got close to the three than Chinna Maruthu Pandiyar kicked one sepoy and Periya Maruthu Pandiyar strangled another with his bare hands. The king dodged and disarmed a third sepoy who tried to bayonet him. He then proceeded to use the same bayonet to stab his attacker and the sepoy who had borne the brunt of Chinna Maruthu Pandiyar's kick right into their chests. The sepoys now lay dead on the ground.

All three men, now armed with English bayonets, rushed into the neighbouring forest. More English sepoys saw them escaping. Rather than chasing them, the sepoys got into position and started firing their muskets in their direction. Upon entering the forest, a stray shot struck the side of Muthuvaduganatha Thevar's face. He collapsed to the ground. After a few moments and with great effort, the wounded king slowly staggered back to his feet. In the commotion, another group of sepoys moved forward into the forest and lunged at the three with their bayonets. Even as the Maruthu brothers fended off multiple sepoys with their own bayonets, two sepoys slashed the king's back as he stood dazed from the shot that had struck his face. Turning around, the now bleeding king bayoneted a sepoy. But the other sepoy was quick to stab him in the gut. Muthuvaduganatha Thevar retaliated by sinking the bayonet deep into the chest of his other attacker. The two sepoys collapsed at the king's feet. But the raja was losing blood fast due to the injuries on his face, gut and back. Seeing the expanding red stain on the king's white vest, Periya Maruthu Pandiyar picked him up, hoisted him on his shoulder and started running deeper into the forest towards their camp. Chinna Maruthu Pandiyar held off the remaining sepoys as his elder brother made his escape.

The older Maruthu brother ran without pausing to catch his breath. After a few minutes, the younger general caught up with them, having managed to give the sepoys the slip. The warm blood gushing from the king's wounds was soaking Periya Maruthu Pandiyar's clothes and turning his vest a deeper shade of red.

Chinna Maruthu Pandiyar looked at his brother and said, 'I will carry him to the camp now.'

Periya Maruthu Pandiyar nodded and carefully shifted the

wounded king, who was losing consciousness, onto his younger brother's shoulders. As the three neared the main camp, they were shocked to see a much larger unit of Arcot and English soldiers surrounding it, with an attack underway. The English sepoys were firing their muskets from one end of the camp, while the Arcot cavalry were hacking their swords at the other. It was clear the Sivaganga soldiers had been ambushed as they were winding down the camp. The element of surprise and the sheer number of the enemy troops had caught the Sivaganga soldiers off guard. They didn't have the time to get into position or the leadership of their best generals, the Maruthu brothers, to rally them and bring them into a defensive formation. The soldiers, despite being scattered across the camp, were fighting bravely with no regard for death or pain. But it was a losing battle. A multitude of shots from the muskets of the English battered the Sivaganga soldiers, while the Arcot cavalry charged on the ones who escaped the musket shots.

The soldiers threw their valaris steadily at their enemies. Each valari took an opponent out, but there were far too many for them to break through. As the Sivaganga ranks thinned, the ambushers made their next move. Tents and supply carts were lit up by the Arcot cavalry and the English sepoys. The remaining soldiers in the middle started choking on a thick cloud of smoke. The battlefield was slowly turning into a scene of massacre.

All through this, the Maruthu brothers stayed out of everyone's sights. Losing all hope, they stepped away from the battle scene to safer grounds. Even while moving away, they could still hear the clashes at the camp and see a thick plume of smoke rising in the air from the battlefield.

Chinna Maruthu Pandiyar feared the worst. He addressed his elder brother, 'The main camp has been ambushed as well. The king won't be safe here. We need to move him to a safer place.'

Before Periya Maruthu Pandiyar could reply, Raja Muthuvaduganatha managed to command his generals in a feeble voice, 'Put me down.'

The king sounded weak, but he was still awake and conscious. He had lost a serious amount of blood. The wounds on his chest and back were deep. Chinna Maruthu Pandiyar carefully laid him down.

The king continued, 'Leave me here. Take Velu and Vellachi to a safe place. Protect them.'

Periya Maruthu Pandiyar didn't heed his king's order.

'We will not leave you, my lord. We will be here, protecting you till our last breath.'

'Peri Pandi, protect the lineage of Sivaganga. You have sworn your loyalty to the kingdom. Protect them for Sivaganga!'

Chinna Maruthu Pandiyar clutched the king's shoulders and spoke earnestly, 'We can't leave you here, my lord. We will carry you back. We will protect our queen, the princess and you. We will not let you die!'

'Leave me here, Chinna Pandi! This is an order!'

The king of Sivaganga stopped talking. He let out all his anger in a burst of heavy breaths. With the rage out of his system, his breathing slowed and he softly said, 'Our enemies will not stop here. They will proceed to Sivaganga. It will not be long before they realize Velu and Vellachi are in Kollangudi. They will not stop until both of them are killed. Take my family away to a safe place. Protect them; protect the lineage.

Time is of the essence and I will only slow you down. Leave me here, please. Protect the future of our kingdom.'

The Maruthu brothers steeled their faces. With a heavy heart, they bowed to their king and began sprinting towards Kollangudi. As the generals moved further away from the battlefield, they came across two stray war horses belonging to the Arcot cavalry, which had escaped the scene of the battle. Grabbing them by their bridles, the Maruthu brothers mounted the horses and raced towards Kollangudi.

4

Post-harvest of 1772, Mariamman Temple, Kollangudi

KOLLANGUDI WAS A TOWN THAT HAD GROWN AROUND THE Mariamman temple. There was nothing here that would have caught the attention of any passing traveller. There were no rich temples or treasuries to entice marauders and no barracks to attract the attention of enemy armies. This was the first safe town outside Sivaganga. Thandavaraya Pillai decided to bring Rani Velu Nachiyar and Princess Vellachi here for their safety, as per the king's instructions before leaving for the war camp. Udaiyal and her team of women bodyguards formed a crucial part of the entourage guarding the royalty.

Upon reaching Kollangudi, the queen made known her wish to offer prayers at the Mariamman temple for the safe return of her husband. The prime minister obliged her request, and soon the queen's entourage was inside the temple.

Despite being a small town, its residents had brightened the streets up with rows of bunting and colourful *kolam* rangolis to welcome the queen and her daughter. There was joy and excitement in the air at the arrival of royalty and, even though their soldiers were just an hour away at Kalayar Koil waging a battle against Arcot and the English, the town was consumed with the spirit of celebration. The residents of Kollangudi were confident in the ability of their army, and they welcomed the queen and her entourage with pomp and grandeur.

Dust rose behind the two horses as they galloped on the dry, thorny terrain towards Kollangudi. With the dust blocking his vision, the town watchman came out of the guard station carrying his stick for a better view. As they got closer, he quickly recognized the Maruthu brothers atop the horses, dropped the stick and ran towards them.

Chinna Maruthu Pandiyar didn't pause for any exchange of pleasantries. His throat had dried up during the long journey. In a hoarse voice, he shouted, 'Where's the prime minister?'

'He is in the Mariamman temple,' the watchman promptly offered.

The generals didn't wait; they took their horses through the narrow streets of Kollangudi towards the temple. At its entrance, they alighted from their horses and, without bothering to untie the English muskets with the bayonets from their backs, entered the temple.

The prime minister came out from the inner sanctum to find the Maruthu brothers walking towards him. Their vests were soaked in what looked like blood and had turned into dirty red from the dust. Bruises and cuts marked their faces and hands.

A stunned Thandavaraya Pillai asked, 'What happened, Chinna Pandi, Peri Pandi?'

Settling his breathing, Chinna Maruthu Pandiyar spoke, 'We were ambushed. The English and Arcot forces attacked us in deceit. Feigning peace, the English used the traitor Ramaswamy to lure our king and army into a deathtrap. Our soldiers couldn't face their onslaught. We need to take the queen and the princess to a safe place immediately. They are not safe here anymore—'

As Chinna Maruthu Pandiyar was interrupted by a coughing fit, an equally exhausted Periya Maruthu Pandiyar continued, 'The English and Arcot will come looking for the queen and the princess soon. They want to extinguish the royal line of Sivaganga.'

Before the prime minister could reply, Rani Velu emerged from the inner sanctum. There was concern in her eyes.

'Where is my husband?' she demanded.

The Maruthu brothers remained silent. They had a lump in their throats. The younger general finally managed to speak. 'We were led into an ambush by traitors within our own ranks. The king was mortally wounded in the attack at the Shiva temple in Kalayar Koil. He asked us to take you and the princess to safety, my queen.'

The rani stood silent.

The town watchman came in, gasping for breath.

'My lord! My lord! A troop of horsemen is heading towards Kollangudi. They don't look like our soldiers!'

Thandavaraya Pillai was the first to react. He called out to his retainer, 'Arrange horses for the queen, her close aides, the princess and the Maruthu generals here. We are leaving now!'

The retainer ran out with his orders. 'Where are we going?' Chinna Maruthu Pandiyar asked.

'We will head northwest towards the territories that are hostile to Arcot. Now, hurry!'

Amid all this commotion, Rani Velu stood frozen. She was in a state of shock. The prime minister came close to her and said in a soft voice, 'We need to leave immediately, my queen. Now is not the time for sorrow. We need to protect the light of Sivaganga. I request you to follow the Maruthu brothers out. We have to take you and the princess to safety.'

Rani Velu Nachiyar merely nodded. Her eyes had welled up. She followed the prime minister's instructions and followed the Maruthu brothers outside.

Thandavaraya Pillai carried the six-year-old princess out of the temple. His retainer had already brought with him a bunch of horses. Close aides of the queen, the Maruthu brothers and Thandavaraya Pillai got on their respective horses. The queen's personal bodyguard, Udaiyal, helped Vellachi onto the horse of a close aide of the queen. Just as she hoisted the princess up, another bodyguard armed Udaiyal with a *maru*, a small, round metal shield with sharp blackbuck horns on its two ends, and an aruval, a sword with a reversed curve at its end, on her back. The other bodyguards of the queen were already armed.

Rani Velu Nachiyar looked curiously at Udaiyal and asked, 'Why aren't you on a horse, Udaiyal?'

'We need to hold back the enemies while you make your escape, my queen. We will stall them. That should give you enough time to escape.'

'No, Udaiyal. You are coming with us,' Velu Nachiyar exclaimed.

Chinna Maruthu Pandiyar cut into the conversation, 'We need to leave now. They are almost here.'

The rani's weak protest was ignored, given the urgency, and the queen's party broke away from the armed group of bodyguards on the ground. They started heading northwest into the dry, bristly forest that was visible on the horizon.

Pulling out the aruval from her back, Udaiyal called in all bodyguards who had stayed behind. They were all women who had broken into the male bastion of armed warfare and had been trained in the ancient arts of silambam for many years. No strangers to a fight, they had a wide array of weapons – kattaris, valaris, dagger, swords, maru and aruvals.

Gripping an aruval with her right hand, Udaiyal proclaimed, 'We have one objective and one objective alone. Put enough space between our queen and the enemies. We may not survive this day, but I want this to be the most glorious day of our lives. After today's battle, our enemies should dread encountering our queen and coming anywhere near Sivaganga again. Let us protect our queen. To battle, my sisters! To battle!'

Even as the camp at Kalayar Koil burned, Ameer-ul-Umara, sitting on his horse, looked a little shaken. This was one of his first close encounters with war. However, it didn't dissuade him from playing big.

Looking at Lieutenant Colonel Bonjour who was right beside him, he said, 'Almost all the soldiers of Sivaganga are here at Kalayar Koil. The fort in Sivaganga will be weakly guarded. We need to move quickly and capture the capital. Once we reach there, we need to get rid of the queen and her daughter. We don't want the line of Muthuvaduganatha Thevar to stay alive. Their elimination will make the absorption of Sivaganga much easier.'

'Yes, your highness,' Bonjour agreed. 'This is the right time to capture Sivaganga. We have nearly finished off its army here. I can send the bulk of my infantry towards the capital.'

'Take my cavalry as well. I don't want to take any chances. I will stay behind and complete the plunder of Kalayar Koil.'

Lieutenant Colonel Bonjour said with a sheepish smile, 'The elite infantry troops of the English and the bulk of your cavalry are more than sufficient to capture the fort of Sivaganga. I would like to stay by your side and assist you during the plunder, while ensuring your safety, your highness. We can't be too sure in these hostile territories.'

'Of course, Bonjour. You should stay behind with me. Our infallible armies will finish the job in Sivaganga for us. They can take the path via Kollangudi to Sivaganga. We shouldn't find a lot of resistance along that path.'

'Yes, your highness.' Bonjour bowed, and left to instruct the officers.

Soon, the English infantry and Arcot cavalry made their way to Sivaganga, leaving behind the burning camp at Kalayar Koil. The English soldiers maintained a steady pace, navigating the thorny bushes on their way. Ameer-ul-Umara's cavalry broke formation, and soon they were ahead of the English foot soldiers. It seemed like they were in a hurry to reach Sivaganga to lay their hands on the loot at the capital before the English.

An hour into the march, the scout of the Arcot cavalry, who was just ahead of the main unit, returned to the general even as they could see Kollangudi at the horizon.

The scout informed the general, 'There seems to be a group of people in a loose formation just outside the town. They are all women. But it looks like they might give us battle.'

The middle-aged general ordered his cavalry to a halt.

'A bunch of women? How many are there? Were they armed?'

'Not many. I think our cavalry alone can outnumber them three times over.'

'Well, then, we will trample them under the hooves of our horses. Speed up! We have some women for ourselves further ahead!' the general commanded his soldiers.

As they moved closer to the town, the troops got a clearer picture of what they were to face. Not more than forty women, lightly armed with aruvals, were standing and shouting aggressively.

The Arcot general didn't have patience for any roadblocks.

'Charge!' he yelled.

There was a fair amount of distance between the two opposing forces and, as the cavalry started charging at full pace, the horses started tiring out and slowing down. Their incursion was petering out.

On the opposite side, despite their numerical disadvantage, the all-women army was spread out strategically to further weaken the impact of the oncoming cavalry charge. As the opponents got closer, the women quickly switched their aruvals for marus and charged at the horses.

Almost all the soldiers of Udaiyal were able to dodge the

horses or tear through the ranks of the troopers with their marus. The horses that got hurt in the process flinched in pain and flung their riders.

The stunned cavalry that went past the women, escaping their marus, turned around to engage them yet again. By then, Udaiyal and her soldiers had already begun taking down the Arcot horsemen at the back and mounting their horses that were unharmed by the marus. Within a few moments, the rear of the Arcot cavalry was taken over by Udaiyal's troops. The Arcot cavalry now had to fight the women on horses. Hand-to-hand combat ensued between the two sides.

The women bodyguards were still outnumbered and surrounded, but they kept slashing the Arcot men, keeping them at bay. The stomping of the horses on the dry ground raised dust, choking everybody and reducing visibility. Nobody inside this huddle could see anything outside.

Just outside the ring of dust, the English infantry made their appearance. Watching the slugfest ahead of them, they quickly got themselves within range to open fire. Closing the ranks into a tight formation, the sepoys got their muskets ready and angled them towards the huddle.

A sepoy stationed behind the English lines blew his bugle. The Arcot general, who was inside the cloud of dust, immediately recognized the sound – English reinforcements had arrived – and shouted, 'Retreat! Retreat!'

The general's bodyguard blew his horn next. Upon hearing the sound, the Arcot horsemen disengaged from Udaiyal and her warriors and came out of the dust ring to locate the English. As soon as they saw the English troops, they galloped towards them for safety.

Udaiyal, assuming that the Arcot cavalry were retreating out of fear, cried, 'The cowards are turning back! Chase them! Kill them all!'

By the time Udaiyal and her troops exited the ring of dust, most of the Arcot cavalry were already behind the English line. Udaiyal didn't realize that the English were in position to attack them. In a frenzy, she raced along with her all-women troops, chasing Arcot's cavalry straight into the line of fire of the English muskets.

A multitude of musket shots whizzed past the women, some striking the horses that they were riding. One after another, the horses under the women collapsed. Udaiyal and her troops didn't know or care if they were hit. They kept charging. Udaiyal was ahead of others as she made contact with the English sepoys. She slashed her sword at any and every sepoy that came her way and found herself deeper into the English lines. Just then a bayonet stabbed her horse, and she was flung off its back, hitting her head on the ground. Everything went black.

Every part of her body was throbbing with pain. Udaiyal couldn't open her eyes. They felt heavy. She couldn't move her head and could barely feel or move her numb hands, which made her think.

My hands and neck are tied.

She tried moving her legs.

Tied.

The pain was dull but throbbing. It was almost as if she had lost sensation in her body and could not control it anymore. She stayed still until the first coherent thought entered her mind.

My queen!

The mere thought of her increased Udaiyal's pain. The throbbing went up manifold, but the thought of the rani consumed her. She put all her effort into trying to open her eyes. Her vision was blurry at first however, after a few painful blinks, Udaiyal could see clearly. It seemed like the world had flipped ninety degrees. Before she could figure out anything, her vision became blurry again. Something warm and wet went into one of her eyes.

Where am I? What happened?

She blinked several more times and realized it was blood that had dripped down into one of her eyes. Seeing some English sepoys and Arcot soldiers walking outside what looked like the Mariamman temple, Udaiyal understood where she had been restrained. There was a burning smell in the air.

'She woke up!' one of the sepoys shouted, pointing at Udaiyal.

She felt a sharp kick to the head and winced in pain.

'Get her up,' someone else called out.

A sepoy propped Udaiyal up. After a while, a bulky man dressed in armour came over to her.

'You are up already. I didn't expect you to wake up so early. I haven't even removed my armour,' the man snickered.

Udaiyal attempted to speak, but her lips felt swollen and numb. She merely looked groggily at him. But her mind was getting sharper by the minute. She recognized the man. He was the general of the Arcot cavalry.

'Get her ready to talk. I will finish my dinner until then. And burn those women and children properly. They still seem to be alive.'

A sepoy splashed her with a bucketful of water. The cold water singed every wound and bruise on her body. But it seemed to bring back some life into her as well. She now had a better bearing of the situation around her.

Many a thatched roof was burning. The English soldiers were throwing bodies into multiple bonfires that had been lit. Udaiyal shivered as a chilly wind swept past her. It was a cool evening, and the soldiers were using the very same bonfires to keep themselves warm. Udaiyal's thoughts were becoming clearer by the minute.

Where are my girls?

She looked around and realized there was nobody around. Even the sepoy who had thrown water at her had vanished. There were no enemy tents in her line of vision. She inferred they must have set up camp within the temple. She looked for familiar faces, but there were none.

I hope my queen is safe. I hope we bought enough time for her to escape safely.

She couldn't look down. The rope around her neck seemed to be tied to something firm. Her legs were tied to her hands from behind.

I need to free myself.

She wriggled her hands but didn't have the strength to move them more energetically. A sharp pain suddenly arose from below her abdomen. Udaiyal stopped moving. She didn't even want to think about what the soldiers might have done to her. Instead, she looked up at the walls of the temple.

Amma, give me strength to set myself free. Give me strength to vanquish my enemies.

With her short prayer, she continued to move her hands and legs to loosen the ropes. After what seemed like an eternity, the ropes were finally getting loose. Right then, the general, an English officer and a group of soldiers started making their way towards her.

The general, who had changed into a silk robe, was having an animated discussion with the English officer who was still in his red-and-white military attire.

'How can a woman and a child vanish into thin air? Velu Nachiyar must be somewhere around here. You need to search more effectively. Comb the region again,' the general commanded.

The English officer seemed to have other concerns. 'But shouldn't we augment our troops for the Sivaganga expedition rather than have them chase people? We are spread quite thin there.'

'We have enough to take the Sivaganga fort,' the general snapped. 'The queen is my biggest worry. If there is one person the people of Sivaganga would rally around, it is Velu Nachiyar. She and her daughter are the last of the Sivaganga rulers. If we want to ensure Sivaganga is safe in our hands, we need to eliminate her. So invest your resources in finding her. We need to get her at the earliest before Prince Ameer-ul-Umara makes his way to Sivaganga. I don't want any embarrassment when his highness is here. Find her, dead or alive.'

Now standing where Udaiyal was confined, the general looked at her with disdain and said, 'So, Udaiyal, the personal bodyguard of Rani Velu Nachiyar, is finally up. You think you did a good job by stalling us so that your queen could escape? I will have your queen's whereabouts right out of your mouth. Where is she?'

Udaiyal looked up to see his face. She wanted to speak, but couldn't. Her swollen lips just wouldn't open.

An Arcot soldier kicked her chest and ordered, 'Answer the general!'

Udaiyal made more effort to move her lips, and after intense exertion, managed to utter, 'Do you think I will tell it to a mongrel like you?'

She spat at him. Her spit mixed with her blood stained the clean white robe of the general.

'You dare spit on me, you whore!'

The general kicked her in the face. He drew his sword and, in one swift move, slashed Udaiyal's neck. Blood started gushing from her neck as she collapsed.

'Chop her head off!' the general roared.

The English officer stood shocked. He tried to reason with the general, 'She was our one possible lead to find Rani Velu Nachiyar, and you killed her!'

'Well, that isn't my problem! Nobody spits on me and stays alive! Now, find the queen!'

The general stomped his way back to the temple. The English officer followed him, while an Arcot soldier took a heavy axe and chopped Udaiyal's head off her body.

Meanwhile, in Kalayar Koil, Ameer-ul-Umara and Lieutenant Colonel Bonjour were sitting in the main tent right outside the Shiva temple. Both were in good spirits, sipping wine.

'The gold we got here is beyond my expectations, Bonjour.

Fifty thousand pagodas! It has more than compensated my effort here.'

'Yes, your highness. I presume I would have the good fortune of enjoying a small portion of it,' Bonjour pronounced timidly.

'Of course! You will receive your fair share. Not to worry, Bonjour. You will have your gold before we leave for Sivaganga.'

'Thank you, your highness.'

'Will we face any resistance, like we did at Kollangudi, before we reach Sivaganga?'

'I don't think so, your highness. I think Kollangudi was the last resistance put up by them. We have already killed most of them here at Kalayar Koil and the remaining soldiers were slain at Kollangudi. In fact, we got rid of a lot of civilians as well. My soldiers informed me that there were a sizeable number fighting alongside the soldiers here. I am half expecting an empty Sivaganga to welcome us. In fact, we can proceed further and attack Ramanathapuram as well. We can secure all the Marava lands in one fell swoop.'

'Well, we were taken by surprise at Kollangudi, and I don't want any more surprises. We should not take any chances and find ourselves in a quagmire so far from home. I am risking my life in this hostile territory. Ensure that Sivaganga is secured before I enter the fort. Once we have Sivaganga, we can proceed to Ramanathapuram.'

'Of course, my highness. I have asked my troops at Kollangudi to secure Sivaganga before we arrive there. I assure you that we will not have any more surprises.'

'Good. With that settled, let's move on to other matters. How do you plan to deal with Major General Smith?'

'If we can capture Sivaganga at the earliest and if you graciously offer the place to the English as you had promised earlier, I believe we can calm his worries. The benefits of capturing Sivaganga will make him look past my act of insubordination. The council at Madras is bound to support me here.'

He paused, doubt clouding his mind. In a low voice, he asked the prince of Arcot, 'Is it fair for me to assume that Sivaganga will be given to the English?'

'I am not a man who fails to keep his word, Bonjour, and you have my word. Sivaganga will be handed over to the English after its capture and placed under my tutelage. After all, Arcot wants to secure its southern frontier. The English at our southern border will only be a source of strength.'

'Thank you, your highness. Sivaganga with an English garrison under your tutelage is a favourable outcome for all parties involved. If we manage to capture Ramanathapuram as well, the council would be ecstatic. I'm sure Major General Smith would be happy as well. After all, it was one of his goals.'

'Good. Let us break camp tomorrow and start our march towards Sivaganga. If everything goes well, we should reach Sivaganga by the evening.'

'Yes, your highness. I will make all the preparations for the march tomorrow.'

'Before you leave, Bonjour, I would like to ask you one more question. I hear Rani Velu Nachiyar and her daughter escaped. Should we be concerned?'

'That should be the least of our worries, your highness. She is nothing but a helpless woman right now. Her army is decimated. Half her citizenry has been killed, and the rest have escaped to the countryside. She is not a threat anymore. She will be captured in no time. I have my men scouring the area.'

Ameer-ul-Umara didn't look convinced. He was beginning to feel overcome with worry.

'Announce a reward for her capture, dead or alive,' the prince said. 'I will also have my assassins look for her. Keep your men on the case until she is found. I know the last light of Sivaganga is flickering, but I want it extinguished as soon as possible.'

5

Post-harvest of 1772, deep in the forests of Dindigul

THE SUN WAS HIGH UP AS THE GROUP OF EXHAUSTED MEN AND women trudged through thorny bushes and shrubs, stirring up dry dust along their way. The trees were bald and offered no shade. There was no trail behind or in front of the group. Princess Vellachi was fast asleep on a horse, with her retainer sitting behind her, guiding the animal. Rani Velu Nachiyar was just ahead on her own horse next to Thandavaraya Pillai's. Terribly worn out, the prime minister looked tired and could barely keep his eyes open. Old age, coupled with the drudgery of traversing the jungles in this heat, had taken a toll on him.

Periya Maruthu Pandiyar, who was at the rear of the group, came forward to speak to his younger brother. 'I think we are relatively safe here. I will head towards Sivaganga incognito, take stock of the latest situation and rendezvous with you later at the camp you are going to set up for the group.'

A tired Chinna Maruthu Pandiyar asked, 'How will you locate us?'

The elder brother replied with a smile, 'I know these forests like the back of my hand. I will find you. Don't worry about me. Take care of our queen and keep proceeding further.'

Periya Maruthu Pandiyar looked at his exhausted queen and her entourage, bid them goodbye, and started riding towards Sivaganga. There was hardly any protest from the fatigued group.

Taking in the collective weariness, the other Maruthu brother suggested, 'Let's stop here for a while. I will continue ahead and find a place to rest.'

With that, he galloped ahead of the group. Nearly an hour passed before he returned to update the retinue: 'I found a pond ahead. We can rest there for some time. We should have just about enough time to reach the next village by dusk.'

Nobody responded. They looked dazed. Chinna Maruthu Pandiyar didn't expect any response either. The group merely followed the man.

The fine clothes worn by the royalty already looked worn out and dirty. Their exquisite silk attires were not designed to withstand the harsh environment. Lack of sleep and the overwhelming fear of being killed amplified the distraught look of the group. The rani had remained silent throughout the escape. She merely followed orders as they got deeper into the forests of Dindigul.

The group reached a small pond. They all stopped by its edge and alighted their horses. Retainers filled their leather skin bags with water while the horses were taken to the far end of the pond for grazing. The queen and other high-ranking officials took the better spot next to the pond, which had flat stones to sit on and rest, while the retinue took to the other end of the pool for a breather.

Thandavaraya Pillai drank from the pond and sat on the stone closest to the water. The young general stood next to him, stretching himself. A still-asleep Vellachi was lying on a flat stone beside a maid. Rani Velu Nachiyar sat on the stone farthest from the water but within hearing distance of the prime minister, who broke the silence, 'It will be a few more days before we reach the citadel of Gopala Nayakar. He has been a good friend of Sivaganga and our king. He will surely offer us refuge. I have identified a few villages that can provide us with safe havens during the course of our journey. I'm hoping Periya Maruthu Pandiyar will join us soon after his mission. Until then, Chinna Maruthu Pandiyar will ensure that the villages are safe beforehand.'

The young Maruthu nodded in agreement.

The queen didn't respond to either of them. She was gazing at the pond, looking completely lost.

Thandavaraya Pillai, determined to get a response from Rani Velu, continued, 'My queen, you have been completely silent since we escaped Kollangudi.'

She looked at Thandavaraya Pillai with a resigned face.

'What do you want me to say, Appa? I have lost everything that I loved and cherished.'

Vellachi, who had just woken up, came to her mother's side. Holding her daughter and caressing her cheeks, Rani Velu Nachiyar spoke between sobs, 'Just when the gods gave me everything a woman could ask for and I began to lead a happy life, they snatched everything away from me. I have been rendered helpless. I can't even protect my own daughter.

She will be safer in your hands than mine. I have nothing to live for now.'

'Please don't say that, my queen. You are still the queen of Sivaganga. We need to tread under your guidance now. You are needed more than ever. We will be orphaned without you,' the prime minister said sincerely.

A wry smile broke on Rani Velu's face.

'What can I do, Appa?' she asked. 'How can I guide *you* when I am directionless? I am a powerless woman running for my life. If the people of Sivaganga are dependent on me, then we are truly defenceless, just as we are here – in the middle of the forest with no way forward.'

Thandavaraya Pillai didn't want his queen to sink deeper into despair. He adopted an encouraging tone, 'Let us get ourselves into safer environs, my queen. We can then think of the next course of action with a calm mind. We should not lose hope.'

Just then, a few villagers turned up at the far end of the pond. They seemed to have brought their cattle for a drink of water in the dry heat. The ever-alert Chinna Maruthu Pandiyar approached them to enquire about their whereabouts. After speaking with them for a few minutes, he came back to report to the queen.

'They are residents of a nearby village. They frequent this pond to quench the thirst of their cattle. They also told me something highly concerning, my queen. The nawab of Arcot has announced a reward for your capture – dead or alive. I think assassins and bounty hunters will be swarming these places soon. I'm not sure if the next village will be safe. I will go ahead of you and ascertain the security of the place. If not, I will find a place where we can rest for the night.'

The villagers were looking curiously at the queen and, once their cattle had had their fill of water, they went back in the direction they had come from.

As Chinna Maruthu Pandiyar started walking towards the horses, the prime minister asked, 'Do we move in the direction of the next village, or should we chart a different course?'

'Stay the course. If we need to change direction, I will be back soon enough to effect the change.'

With a wave of goodbye, the general exited into the forest in the same direction as the villagers.

The prime minister ordered the retainers and the queen's maids to prepare for travel. Within half an hour, everyone was ready, and the group continued their march through the forest.

The slow walk through the forest continued until dusk. Nothing in the terrain changed. The shrubs, the thorny bushes, the bald trees – there was not a soul in sight. Just as the sun was setting, Chinna Maruthu Pandiyar reunited with the group. He was accompanied by a small number of villagers, mostly women. They seemed an excited lot.

On seeing the queen, they immediately ran to her and bowed in front of her horse.

Chinna Maruthu Pandiyar ignored the prostration of the villagers. 'The village ahead is not safe. Ameer-ul-Umara's men had visited that place earlier today. It may be filled with informants.'

The rani blessed the villagers and asked, 'Who are these people, Chinna Pandi?'

'These are the family members of people who were working for our king. They are from the villages further north. I visited those places while seeking a safe haven for us. They wanted to accompany me and be under your protection, my queen. I brought them along in the hopes that they could help us navigate the forest since they know the region well.'

There was utmost trust in the eyes of the villagers as they squatted in front of their queen. Their faith in the queen was palpable.

Witnessing this, the queen was at a loss for words.

How can a woman who has lost everything and is running for her own life protect them? Why this blind trust in me? What do they see in me?

Looking at the villagers, she was suddenly reminded of the words Muthuvaduganatha Thevar had spoken to her before leaving for the war. The queen had an epiphany.

They believe the queen of Sivaganga to be their protector, no matter the circumstances. They find solace in the presence of their queen. The queen of Sivaganga is responsible for her people. It's her responsibility to keep this belief strong and intact. I need to live up to the faith they have placed in me. I need to be the queen they seek.

A rare smile spread over Rani Velu Nachiyar's face.

'The rani of Sivaganga will protect her people,' she announced decidedly.

There was an eruption of joy amongst the villagers on hearing their queen affirm their faith.

'Where will we spend the night, Chinna Pandi?' she asked, a renewed sense of hope and purpose filling her up.

'Their villages are quite far off from here and we will not be able to reach them as it is almost nightfall. We need to make alternative arrangements. The villagers can help us.'

One villager excitedly offered, 'There is a good flat ground with big rocks for shelter, half an hour from here, eastwards. We will be safe there. I can guide you there, my queen.'

The rani nodded and Chinna Maruthu Pandiyar declared, 'Alright, let's start moving so we can reach those grounds before it gets too dark.'

There was a sprightly enthusiasm in the now larger group as they quickly started their walk.

Within a half hour, they reached the flat grounds. The villagers and the queen's staff quickly got into action and constructed the camp. As night arrived, a campfire was set up. Gruel was prepared using broken rice that some of the villagers had brought along. The young Vellachi was already asleep on a maid's lap. The prime minister was chalking out a plan for the next few days with his general and the queen, 'The village of Chieftain Gopal Nayakar is our last hope now. He has been our ally and is under no obligation to Arcot or the English. I have no doubt that he will help us in our hour of need. His village is still a few days away. With the spies and informants swarming all over the place, we will have to be more cautious about where we stay, where we halt and where we move. We may have to take a circuitous route. This may prolong our suffering, but we will still be alive.'

Chinna Maruthu Pandiyar tried to assure the group, 'I will ensure that we are on the safest path possible at all times.'

'Thank you, Chinna Pandi,' the queen said. 'We are going through deep forests on quite a winding path to reach Gopal Nayakar's village. Will Peri Pandi find his way, evading the Arcot and English soldiers? I hope he returns safely.'

Chinna Maruthu Pandiyar responded with a tinge of

arrogance in his voice. 'I have yet to see a man who can lay a finger on my big brother. I assure you he will return safe and sound from his mission in Sivaganga, my queen. I am awaiting some good news from him, too, in this sea of despair.'

The queen smiled and nodded at Chinna Maruthu Pandiyar. Looking at the tiredness in her prime minister's eyes, she said, 'Let us get some rest tonight. It has been a hard day for us all, and we have harder days to overcome. We need to conserve the energies of our body and mind to conquer them.'

Thandavaraya Pillai welcomed this gesture from the queen and slowly walked to his designated rock to sleep. Rani Velu headed to her spot, where Vellachi was already fast asleep, while Chinna Maruthu Pandiyar sat near the bonfire. After a few minutes, the bonfire went out, and he too went to sleep on the flat ground.

Except for the odd sounds of the wild animals, there was silence and tranquillity all around the camp. Everyone was sound asleep. The men on the night watch were exhausted from the taxing escape and, a few moments later, fell into a deep slumber. Darkness engulfed the whole area.

Meanwhile, a man covered in a thick blanket from head to toe entered the grounds in absolute silence. He stealthily walked from one rock to another, looking at the person sleeping beside each. The man was searching for someone in particular. He suddenly stopped midway, staring straight ahead at a small enclosure formed by two large rocks. It seemed he had found the person he was seeking – Velu Nachiyar.

He moved quickly, bypassing the other rocks in his way. As he got closer to the rani, he removed a kattari from under his blanket. He paused for a moment, trying to confirm that the woman sleeping was indeed the queen of Sivaganga.

She is the queen, he thought to himself.

Gripping his kattari tightly, he bent down to plunge it into her neck.

Just as he bent down, a girl, no more than ten years old, grabbed his leg, tripping him over to the side. The girl kept her firm grip on his leg intact, immobilizing him even as he fell with a loud noise. The man quickly regained his bearings and slashed the girl's right hand with his kattari. She cried out loudly but didn't let go. In all this commotion, Rani Velu Nachiyar woke up and, seeing the assassin, quickly got up and armed herself with the dagger hidden in her saree. Chinna Maruthu Pandiyar had already flung himself onto the assassin and wrapped a huge arm around his neck. Twisting the man's hand, he disarmed him and pulled the assassin away. A retainer lit a torch and brought it near the two.

The general roared, 'Who are you? Who sent you here?'

The assassin cowered. His behaviour seemed out of the ordinary for a professional assassin. He was trembling with fear.

'I am just a bounty hunter. There is a price on the queen's head put up by the Arcot prince. I just did it for the bounty. Please spare my life. I beg you,' he spoke timidly.

'How did you find us?' Chinna Pandi demanded.

'The villagers who saw you at the pond told me that the queen was in this area. I was scouring the place and found your location. Please spare my life.'

Chinna Maruthu Pandiyar responded by plunging the bounty hunter's kattari into his chest. Letting the man drop, he addressed the shocked rani, 'My queen, the party of villagers that joined us didn't know that the people of the nearby village had already sighted you. Had they known, they would have guided us to a safer place, I'm certain. This was a tactical mistake that could have turned fatal, for which I take full responsibility. For now, I shall remain awake and ensure that we are safe for the rest of the night.' He bowed his head.

The rani heaved a sigh of relief. She looked at the little girl whose bravery had just saved her. Blood was dripping from a deep gash on her right hand.

'Oh my God!' the queen exclaimed and quickly stepped towards the girl. She used her dagger to cut a piece of cloth from her red silk saree. Wiping the wound gently, she tied the torn silk cloth around it.

'My brave child. I live today because of you. You put your life at risk for me. I am indebted to you. What is your name, little one?'

The girl had a broad smile on her face, despite her wound. 'Kuyili,' she chirped.

'Kuyili, who are your parents? Where are you from?'

'My father works in Sivaganga for the king. I live in Pasangarai with my relatives.'

'What about your mother?'

'I have no mother,' the girl said softly. 'She is dead. My brothers and I were in our field with our mother when wild boars attacked us. She protected us by killing the wild boars, but she passed away later from the wounds. I wanted to protect you like my mother protected us.' Her mouth curved into a faint smile.

A villager came over to the child and chided her, 'You need to address our queen with respect, Kuyili.'

Kuyili's face shrank at the chiding. Seeing this, the rani pulled the girl towards her and had her sit on her lap.

'She is my child. She needs to give me the respect a child gives her mother. Kuyili, I am your mother from now on. You can call me Amma,' the queen pronounced, smiling widely at her.

The broad smile came back on Kuyili's face. Sensing her hesitation, Rani Velu reached out and hugged the little girl. Kuyili hugged her back.

'Amma,' she said fondly.

The next morning, the group continued their journey. With the help of the villagers, Chinna Maruthu Pandiyar was able to find a safe village for the group. By late afternoon, they were in Sanarpatti. In the midst of civilization at last, they were offered food and comfortable thatched huts to stay in. Everyone had retired to their huts in the evening. As the sky turned red, Periya Maruthu Pandiyar entered the village on the back of his horse. The rider and the horse looked exhausted and worn out.

The villagers helped the older Maruthu brother off his horse and offered him water.

'Where is the queen?' he enquired.

'She is resting in the hut ahead,' one of the villagers answered.

Gulping down the water, he walked to the hut the villager had pointed at. A retainer outside the hut allowed him to enter. Rani Velu Nachiyar was sitting against the wall farthest from the entrance, with Thandavaraya Pillai to her right and Chinna Maruthu Pandiyar to her left. On seeing him, a gleaming Rani

Velu jumped to her feet and exclaimed, 'Peri Pandi, it's so good to see you! I hope you can bring us a ray of light in this time of darkness.'

The older general bowed before the queen. There was nothing but sadness on his face. His grim look wiped the smile off the rani's face. Concerned, she asked, 'What has happened, Peri Pandi? Are things worse than we fear?'

'It is my misfortune that I bear only terrible news, my queen,' he said dejectedly. 'The English officer Lieutenant Colonel Bonjour and the Prince Ameer-ul-Umara marched on to Sivaganga after defeating our army at Kalayar Koil. The morale in Sivaganga was broken after our defeat. To avoid further bloodshed, the citizens and the soldiers vacated the fort and disappeared into the neighbouring villages. Our enemies faced no resistance. They occupied the fort.'

Rani Velu Nachiyar closed her eyes. The general continued, 'I visited the place incognito. Prince Ameer-ul-Umara has handed over the place to the English. They are stockpiling arms and ammunition and also maintaining a garrison there. A large chunk of the English army has started moving towards Ramanathapuram. The prince has left for Arcot, leaving behind most of his army at Kalayar Koil. The rest are spread all across our kingdom. He has announced a bounty on your head, my queen. There are a lot of Arcot and English soldiers looking for you in Sivaganga.'

The queen simply nodded, her face troubled.

'I went back to Kalayar Koil looking for our king,' Periya Maruthu Pandiyar said, his voice quivering.

Velu Nachiyar held her breath.

'I could not find him,' he said softly, cutting the silence. 'Almost everybody in Kalayar Koil has been killed or maimed. Most of the houses were burnt. There was still a stench of dead people in the air, even though it had been many days since the battle.'

The queen heaved a sigh of resignation. She then asked, 'What about Udaiyal and my bodyguards? They stayed back in Kollangudi to stall the Arcot army.'

Periya Maruthu Pandiyar couldn't meet the queen's eyes. He merely kept his head down. He tried to speak, but he choked; words evaded him. After a few moments and with great difficulty, he managed to speak. 'If it was not for Udaiyal, we would have never escaped our enemies. She fought with valour and grit. I have seen few men who are as brave as her. She nearly vanquished the Arcot cavalry and bought us enough time to make our escape.' The general paused.

Rani Velu feared the worst.

'Is she alive?'

'No, my queen.'

Periya Maruthu Pandiyar wouldn't lift his head.

'Are you hiding something from me, Peri Pandi?' the queen demanded.

He lifted his head. His eyes were red; tears rolled down his cheeks. He clenched his jaw. Reigning in his anger, he spoke, 'Those sons of whores defiled and tortured Udaiyal. They tried to extract our whereabouts from her, but she wouldn't reveal our location. She didn't yield to their torture. Out of spite, those bastards chopped off her head and hung it on a pole outside Kollangudi. I only pray that I live long enough to rip their guts out and drink their blood. Only then will I have lived my life justly. I failed to protect our king. I failed to protect our women. I failed Sivaganga!' The large man broke down.

Rani Velu Nachiyar who had been standing motionless all this while, began moving towards Periya Maruthu Pandiyar. Thandavaraya Pillai and Chinna Maruthu Pandiyar also stood up. She gestured for them to stay behind. Coming over to the older Maruthu brother, she gently patted his arms with sisterly affection. She then stepped out of the hut.

Outside, a few villagers had stacked logs to make a pyramid and lit them to make a bonfire. Velu Nachiyar looked at the growing fire as it rose. Her face was grim, but there was fervour in her eyes.

Brave, honourable men and women have given their lives for Sivaganga. They have endured the worst of our enemy to protect me. Little Kuyili was ready to lay down her life for me. My ever-loyal Udaiyal has already sacrificed herself. My beloved husband has been martyred for the same cause. I cannot let their sacrifices be in vain. In this hour of despair, my people still believe in me. I cannot let them down. I need to rise. I need to rise for Sivaganga, for my people, for the fallen. I need to rise for my love.

Rani Velu Nachiyar took out her bejewelled hair clip. Her lush hair swayed gently in the breeze. She looked ominous standing next to the cracking bonfire.

I will take back Sivaganga!

6

Post-harvest of 1772, Virupatchi

VIRUPATCHI, FOR ALL PRACTICAL PURPOSES, WAS A FOREST IN the province of Dindigul. Some huts and a few agricultural fields gave it the semblance of a village. A large hill protected the place from the south, and a couple of smaller hills formed its eastern and western boundaries. The deciduous trees were bald in the summer, but their sheer volume was enough to keep the area isolated from the larger civilization. Reaching this concealed location undoubtedly required effort. In the middle of this remote village was a large dwelling.

Gopal Nayakar's two-storeyed house, with broad steps in the middle leading to the first floor, welcomed Rani Velu Nachiyar and her group. At the bottom of the steps, the host stood waiting to greet the rani and her people. He was a short man, with a slightly pronounced paunch, and a thick white moustache covering his mouth, which drew attention away from his bald head. His fearsome reputation was clearly not based on his external appearance, which was anything but intimidating.

'Welcome, my queen! Welcome to my humble abode,' he said with folded hands.

That morning, he had sent a small contingent of his big, burly retainers to escort their visitors to the village. Once the queen of Sivaganga and her entourage reached a point near the building, the retainers helped everybody get off their horses. Rani Velu greeted her host, 'You are the succour to our tired souls. I thank you for offering us shelter and hospitality, Gopal Nayakar.'

'It's nothing if not my duty. We have made arrangements for everyone here. I thank you for accepting my hospitality, my queen,' he replied.

The arduous journey was finally over, and they made themselves at home. Vellachi, who had fallen ill on the way, was immediately taken to the local doctors for treatment at the queen's request.

Later that night, after a sumptuous meal, the rani, along with the prime minister and the Maruthu brothers, was sitting in their host's personal quarters. Chinna Maruthu Pandiyar had prepared a special *thambulam* meal.

'Chinna Pandi has apprised me of the present situation. I am willing to offer any assistance within my capacity, my queen,' Gopal Nayakar offered.

'Thank you, Gopal. Would your overlord be upset if you assist me? I don't want to get you into any trouble just to alleviate my suffering.'

'There is nothing to worry about, my queen. In fact, the authorities at Dindigul would encourage any action against Arcot.'

Rani Velu Nachiyar felt a sense of relief. Slowly a look of determination replaced the worry on her face.

'Let me cut to the chase, Gopal. I want to take back

Sivaganga. For that, I require people, arms, ammunition, money and supplies.'

The chieftain looked dumbfounded and said, 'My queen, with all due respect, I am merely the feudal leader of a small area. I could hardly provide the means for—'

'I am not expecting all our needs to be met by you, Gopal,' Velu Nachiyar interjected. 'We simply need your assistance in procuring them. I am requesting you to allow us to set up a base here while we raise an army and gather supplies. Your support, in terms of men and arms, as we make the push for Sivaganga will be more than enough. Assure us that you will be by our side during this onerous journey.'

Gopal Nayakar got up and came towards Rani Velu Nachiyar. Touching her feet, he said, 'I assure you of my unflinching loyalty. All my men and resources are at your disposal. You will exercise a greater right than me over the lands I control for as long as it takes to get back Sivaganga. I promise all my support and energies to your cause, my queen. I am indebted to your husband and his father for all that I have achieved today. Nothing that I do now will be enough to repay what they have done for me.'

'Thank you, Gopal,' the queen said, holding back tears.

There was a pause in the conversation as the group went for another round of thambulam. Gopal Nayakar broke the monotony with a question.

'What is your plan of action now, my queen?'

Rani Velu was patient with the betel leaves in her mouth. She took her time before replying.

'A lot of our citizens are spread across Sivaganga and in hiding. I will have Peri and Chinna Pandi enlist all the able men and get them combat-ready. Appa will work with creditors to procure money for the campaign. He will also engage with our allies to solicit support against Arcot and the English. Gopal, I would like you to look after supplies, arms and ammunition for the people we enlist in our new army.'

Everyone nodded enthusiastically while listening to the queen's proposal. Chinna Maruthu Pandiyar asked, 'How would you like us to proceed with our duty? We need your guidance, my queen.'

'Peri Pandi mentioned that our people fled to the neighbouring villages after the attack on Sivaganga. I would like you and Peri Pandi to visit as many villages and towns as possible in order to identify our people. We will set up base in Virupatchi, with help from Gopal Nayakar. You should bring them here and train whomever you can. This task can't be done overnight, and it requires a lot of effort. You need to inspire people to fight for Sivaganga again, reinstate hope in them. I am looking to both of you to rebuild our army.'

Almost concluding the rani's ask, Periya Maruthu Pandiyar said, 'And we will rebuild the army!'

Rani Velu looked at Thandavaraya Pillai. 'Appa, we need money to sustain this new army. We have lost everything. I hope our creditworthiness amongst the bankers still holds good. I am relying on you to meet our monetary needs.'

The prime minister began briefing the queen, 'I have sent across messages today to various bankers, my queen. I will not let you down. I have also written to various palegars and nayakas within Arcot and in the Marava countries, asking them to stand with us in our fight against our enemies. We need to convince them that we fight the righteous cause and, more importantly, the winning cause. Our standing has taken a hit with our defeat. We need to put in additional effort to win them over to our side.'

'I trust you will overcome all their doubts and misgivings and shore up our numbers, Appa,' the queen said confidently.

Turning to Gopal Nayakar, the rani continued, 'We need food to feed our army. We are not in control of our own lands, and yet we need food grains and other supplies for sustenance. You know the terrain well. I want you to secure lines of supplies for the base that we set up here.'

The chieftain accepted his assignment with a respectful nod.

With everyone assigned a task, it was time to call it a day. The queen patiently finished her food while others waited on her. Finishing the delicious stimulant prepared by Chinna Maruthu Pandiyar, the rani said, 'Alright, I will retire to my quarters now. We will begin working on our plan tomorrow.'

With her exit from the room, the other attendees, too, retired to their respective assigned quarters.

The next morning, Rani Velu was up early. After spending some time in Vellachi's quarters, enquiring about her daughter's health with the doctors and tending to her, she walked down the stairs outside to see the Maruthu brothers and their horses getting ready. The ostlers were loading bags onto the horses while the Maruthu brothers remained deep in discussion. Upon seeing the queen come out, they greeted her. Velu Nachiyar returned their greetings.

'Where are you two headed from here?'

Chinna Maruthu Pandiyar spoke on their behalf. 'We are heading in two directions, my queen. We figured we can cover more ground in a shorter span of time if we split up. I am heading south and my brother will head east. We will return to the base multiple times, as and when we enlist men from different villages. This will ensure that we have a steady stream of people coming here for training.'

'I trust your decision, Chinna Pandi. May God be with you. I will a wait your safe return and hopefully some much-needed good news.'

By now, the horses were ready. The Maruthu brothers bowed down and touched the queen's feet. With her blessing, they mounted their horses and headed out.

Velu Nachiyar headed up the stairs to find the prime minister talking to Gopal Nayakar in the main hall of the house and seemed to be dressed for travel. Seeing the queen enter the main hall, he bowed to her and began, 'I need to head to our neighbouring Marava kingdom, Ramanathapuram. The English have been attacking the palegars and nayakas there for some time now. A personal visit to these chieftains would help us win them over against the English. I will be taking a few retainers along with your permission, my queen.'

A worried rani replied, 'Appa, it's too dangerous to venture into hostile territories with just a few retainers. I would urge you to either write to them or send someone else to convey your message. Your age and deteriorating health will not permit you to make such a hazardous journey.'

'In this hour of need, my personal appearance is even more essential to convince these chieftains. We are seeking help and alliances not from a position of power, but as defeated rulers, and nobody likes to associate themselves with defeated people. We need all the tact and diplomacy at our disposal to win them over. We do not have many accomplished diplomats in our fold right now. I need to make this travel, my queen. I humbly request that you allow me to make this journey,' the prime minister said with folded hands.

Velu Nachiyar clasped his two hands. 'You are invaluable, Appa. I cannot afford to lose you too. I don't want to commit the sin of sending you into the jaws of death. I implore you to stay back.' The fear of losing her father-figure was looming large over the queen.

'I will steer clear of harm's way, my queen. For your satisfaction, I will go incognito. I will be back safe and sound. Please allow me to fulfil my duties towards Sivaganga.'

The queen was grappling with too many losses and emotions.

I feared that I had lost everything when I lost my husband. But Appa has remained my source of strength. He didn't let me sink in despair. I owe it all to him. I am scared of sinking back into the depths of anguish if I lose him. But Appa is adamant. His determination to win back our kingdom is stronger than mine and, as he said, he is the best person to influence our allies to fight for our cause. I need to give in. I need to steel myself. I need to be stronger.

She conceded defeat.

'Alright, Appa. I trust your decision. But please do take more retainers along. Your safety is paramount to me.'

'As you wish, my queen. Thank you for trusting my judgement.'

'I wish you success in this endeavour.'

'Thank you. With your permission, I will return to my personal quarters and finish a few last-minute chores before leaving for my journey.'

Rani Velu Nachiyar obliged his request with a heavy heart.

Thandavaraya Pillai left the main hall as Gopal Nayakar took over the conversation.

'I would also like to request your permission to leave, my queen. I am planning to meet some merchants who can help us with supplies for our base. I need to do this clandestinely, lest we reveal our plans to the English and the nawab. I will be going incognito as well.'

'Of course. I look forward to receiving good news on that front,' the queen said, dismissing the last of her party.

Post-monsoon of 1773, Virupatchi

A large area of land had been cleared out in front of Gopal Nayakar's mansion. There were scores of men training with their silambam sticks. Over the last few months, a lot more huts had been erected further north of the pitch. A bunch of women were working in the fields, with Vellachi – who was now fully recovered – helping them.

The Maruthu brothers were in charge of training men whom they had recruited for the new army. The chieftain and the queen were standing in the balcony of the former's house, watching the men in action.

Seeing his face clouded with worry, the queen asked, 'Gopal, you seem down. Please tell me what troubles you.'

He replied with some hesitation, 'We have men now, my queen. But, most of them are villagers who have been inspired to fight for you. And we still don't have enough numbers to mount a proper attack. The Arcot and the English armies are much better equipped, and their soldiers are much better trained than ours.'

'Our men are brave,' Velu Nachiyar said with conviction.

'I never questioned their bravery, my queen,' he replied. 'But we need more than that to take on our enemies. We are on our own. None of our allies are willing to back us on the battlefield. All we got from them were mere words and hollow promises.'

'We'll have to overcome on our own then,' she said matter-of-factly.

'The grain merchants are charging a premium for the staples,' the chieftain continued. 'Our credit runs low and, hence, they have jacked up the prices. It's nearly impossible to mount a campaign without enough food or money.'

The queen remained silent and continued looking at her worried host as he continued listing his concerns.

'We don't have enough iron to forge more weapons. We don't have the money to procure more metal. We don't have enough blacksmiths. None of the merchants want to deal with us out of their fear of the English. How will we get back Sivaganga with so many handicaps?'

Velu Nachiyar smiled, looking at Gopal Nayakar's worried face.

'Let's deal with them one by one,' she said tenderly.

She looked out at the women working with their sickles and continued, 'Our women are as brave and strong as our men. The same blood that flows through the veins of our soldiers also flows through them. They are the mothers, sisters, wives and daughters of our soldiers. They have the same courage engrained in them. With the right guidance, they will be as strong as our men. There are almost as many women as men here. Let us train our women in the ancient martial arts of silambam. We will double the size of our army.'

'But, my queen—'

Rani Velu Nachiyar cut him short. 'It was my brave Udaiyal and her girls who saved me. They were no different from the girls you see down there. With proper training, we will have an army of Udaiyals that can strike fear in the hearts of our enemies.'

Inspired by her own epiphany, she continued animatedly, 'I will have the Maruthu brothers raise an army of women. We shall train the women the same way as we are training our men. Until now, we only had a women's battalion of bodyguards. But from here on, we will have an entire army comprised of women. They will be as valiant as our Udaiyal.'

The memories of the ultimate sacrifice made by Udaiyal flooded the rani's thoughts.

I will not let the Udaiyal's martyrdom go in vain. Her sacrifice will not be forgotten. The legacy of Udaiyal must live on. She must be remembered by one and all.

'I will call this army of trained women Udaiyal,' she declared. 'That's the least I can do for her memory and sacrifice.'

She looked at the feudal leader. 'So, now the problem is no longer the number of troops we have at our disposal. The challenge now is how we train them. I will have some silambam trainers hired to teach our girls the ancient art.'

Gopal Nayakar accepted the queen's assertion with no further questions. His faith in her always surpassed his scepticism.

'Now, coming to the problem of the lack of iron and money for arms and ammunition – we will have to work within our means,' Velu Nachiyar went on. 'We will concentrate our efforts on forging valaris rather than long swords. This should reduce the consumption of iron for each weapon. Our blacksmiths are adept at forging valaris and can churn out more weapons this way. This will help us equip ourselves with arms very soon. We will have our women trained in the art of using valaris as well. We must put the fear of our traditional weapons in the hearts of those unscrupulous English.'

The chieftain nodded, considering the queen's quick solutions to all his concerns. She continued. 'Lastly, as for the lack of allies and supplies, I have utmost faith in Appa and you to overcome these challenges.'

Gopal Nayakar bowed down to her with folded hands. 'I am humbled and honoured by your faith in me, my queen.'

'We will not make any moves until you tell us that our supplies are sufficient,' the queen reassured him. 'We will wait until Appa's return to discuss the next course of action in building alliances with other kingdoms.'

Rani Velu called on the Maruthu brothers from the balcony to discuss her plan.

The Maruthu brothers came over running.

'Yes, my queen,' they said in unison.

'Peri Pandi, Chinna Pandi, Gopal and I have been discussing about enlarging the size of our army. I have proposed that we train the women in warfare so that they may augment the present troops.'

There was nothing but excitement in the eyes of Periya Maruthu Pandiyar.

'That's a brilliant proposal, my queen,' he said. 'Our womenfolk are imbued with courage and strength.'

Velu Nachiyar nodded before saying, 'Train them in the art of using the silambam and valari. I urge you to take the lead. Recruit as many silambam and valari trainers as you need for this task. We need our girls to be combat-ready as soon as possible.'

'That will be an honour, my queen. I will scout the lands and employ as many trainers as possible,' Periya Maruthu Pandiyar vowed.

Within the next few weeks, enough trainers were brought to Virupatchi, and the women replaced their sickles with silambam sticks and valaris. They began their training on the field right next to the one where the men were. Soon, they became proficient in wielding traditional weapons and learned the general methods of warfare.

Meanwhile, to equip their growing army, Chinna Maruthu Pandiyar worked with the blacksmiths to switch from forging swords to making valaris. He also managed to hire a few more blacksmiths for this purpose. With the additional blacksmiths, who specialized in forging valaris, there was a buzz in the forge as they produced more and more valaris by the day.

The Maruthu brothers continued making trips to villages and towns far and wide to enlist more men and women for their cause. There was a steady trickle of people into Virupatchi. The army under Rani Velu Nachiyar grew day by day. But there was still one important cog missing – Thandavaraya Pillai. He still hadn't returned from his mission.

A few more weeks later, the prime minister returned to Virupatchi. There was no elation on his face. His health had also deteriorated considerably. The rani wouldn't allow a debrief from him until his health recouped.

A few days later, while returning from her morning exercise routine with the Udaiyal army, she found Thandavaraya Pillai in the main hall waiting for her. He looked much better than the day he had arrived, but his journey seemed to have taken an irreparable toll on him as he still looked fatigued.

The queen approached him warmly. 'Appa, you are up early today and already out of your quarters. This is a pleasant surprise.'

Bowing gently to greet her, the prime minister said, 'We need to talk about my mission, my queen. I am afraid I do not carry much good news.'

'Let's talk in my personal quarters,' the queen said, seeing the downcast look on his face.

They proceeded to the rani's quarters, with the queen supporting the fatigued old man.

The rani had him sit in a chair while she took the one across from him. Thandavaraya Pillai began, 'The English have moved quickly through Marava country. They have either already bought off or defeated the local chieftains in the region. They have spread their tentacles everywhere. Ramanathapuram was safe under your father's rule. But now, your cousin who broke away from the alliance we built between Sivaganga and Ramanathapuram after your marriage, has been defeated by the English. He has been captured and Ramanathapuram is now under the control of the English. I spoke with most of the palegars and nayakas of the Marava country. There is a deep resentment towards the English but the local leaders have also been cowed into silence and do not want to be seen openly opposing their far more powerful overlords. Most of them sympathize with our situation but the best they can offer is goodwill alone. A few have offered a token number of soldiers; however, there is hardly anybody who is willing to join our cause to take back Sivaganga from the English. We are all alone, my queen.

Rani Velu Nachiyar didn't let her disappointment show, seeing how close the prime minister was to breaking down. She replied gently, 'I understand, Appa. We have been facing issues with supplies as well. The English are isolating us politically and economically. They are sparing no options to eliminate us.'

The prime minister continued after a long pause, 'Most of the palegars are unable to support us monetarily as well. The scale of our demand is beyond their means. Until we launch a full-fledged campaign, by way of which we offer a credible challenge to the English, I don't think the palegars will join us. I am quite sceptical about them joining our cause at all. They lack confidence in our ability to take on the combined forces of Arcot and the English. They are hedging their risks, but are mostly leaning towards the side of our enemies.'

Velu Nachiyar continued listening quietly. Thandavaraya Pillai said in grim conclusion, 'For the moment, we are essentially on our own.'

'I understand, Appa. We will need to address this problem in due course. Right now, I have a more urgent issue. We are running short of supplies for sustaining the army. I would like to sustain this army as it stands before increasing its numbers further.'

'What are the challenges we're confronted with in procuring additional supplies, my queen? Is there a lack of credit?'

'Yes, Appa. That is one reason. The greed of the merchants and their exploitation of us in these dire times is another. They know full well how helpless we are and have increased the prices of essential supplies significantly, citing our bad credit. We're not left with many sources to generate revenue anyway. So, it is extremely difficult to get credit from bankers or merchants. Then there is the general fear of the English, which dissuades most merchants, whom we have known for decades, from selling supplies to us.'

The prime minister sank deeper into the chair with a sigh of defeat. He then added, 'While we are pinned down here with no men or supplies, the English have been aggressive in pushing their territorial boundaries further south, neutralizing all our potential allies.'

'How are they able to move so far from Madras? How are they feeding their army?'

'They are procuring rice and other supplies from Thanjavur. The Marathas there actively support the English cause,' the prime minister replied, shaking his head in disappointment.

Rani Velu Nachiyar stood up from her chair and started pacing up and down the room.

'I think we can get our supplies from an alternative source, Appa,' she said, breaking the silence. 'If the English have been obtaining their supplies from Thanjavur for their campaign down south, then their supply lines must be stretched thin, and these lines must pass through Virupatchi. If we're able to discern a weak spot, we could attack it and steal their supplies. Our army has been training hard. This exercise will also give them a much-needed battle experience, albeit a small one. We might also be able to augment our supplies at the enemy's expense. What do you think, Appa?'

Thandavaraya Pillai instantly stood up with a broad smile on his face.

My queen is back!

'I think this might work, my queen.'

Before the onset of winter, 1773, somewhere between Madurai and Sivaganga

A small line of bullock carts carrying some English sepoys was moving along a well-marked trail through the dry forest between Madurai and Sivaganga. The forest did not offer much cover and the sepoys were fast asleep in their carts.

One of the sepoys in the leader cart suddenly woke up and brought the entire line to a stop.

'Hey! Wake up!' he called out to his fellow soldiers. 'Is it me or do you too see two women ahead of us?'

His words woke everybody up.

'Women? Where?' one of them asked a little groggily.

The sepoys saw two thin women, no more than twenty years old, dressed in identical maroon sarees, standing a few hundred metres ahead on the trail. Without warning, a few flying metal valaris hit some of the carts. Some of them injured the sepoys, others crippled the bullocks. The cattle started moving helter-skelter. They couldn't move much with the heavy load behind them, but with the bullocks trying to break free, a few carts toppled over. The women had now vanished.

The sepoys who were fortunate enough to escape the attack of the valaris unscathed, picked up their swords and hopped out of their carts. Almost on cue, a legion of aruval-bearing soldiers, surged from behind the bullock carts.

In a matter of a few minutes, all the sepoys were massacred. A large group of valari-clad women corralled all the bullock carts. Humming a song, they unloaded supplies from the broken carts and started carrying them away to Virupatchi. The men took hold of the carts that were still intact and drove them in the same direction as the women.

'Today has been a good haul,' the general of the new army announced. 'I think we are ahead of the group that attacked the English lines from Pudukkottai. Let's keep the momentum up, people. We need to get the honours from the queen.'

Before the onset of winter, 1773, the Arcot palace

An agitated Ameer-ul-Umara was seething in his court in Arcot.

'I went easy on you. She first went after your supplies, then mine and now she has gone a step ahead and started killing my men in the outposts! You should have finished her off when we captured Sivaganga but you didn't. You spent your time and effort on garrisoning the fort and hoarding ammunition rather than searching for her. Now, she is attacking us at our weakest spots and gaining strength from her loots day by day. We can't let this continue. I will look like a fool if I can't put a stop to her actions. I want this to end before her shenanigans grow more detrimental. I want her killed before things get out of hand, Major General Smith!'

The officer stood calmly as he assured the prince of Arcot,

'Yes, your highness. We will devote more of our resources to locate Rani Velu Nachiyar and her army.'

'Not just locate, I want her killed. Find out where she is hiding and exterminate her and her minions. If she continues these attacks, it won't be long before she gets emboldened and plans bigger raids against us. We may lose control of all our southern provinces. Our control over Sivaganga is at stake. My reputation is at stake!'

'We will devote all our resources south of Trichy to smoke out the rebel queen, your highness. I would request you to increase the reward for the head of Velu Nachiyar. I will personally influence the council in Madras to push more funds towards this endeavour. We will recruit more spies, find her hideout and use our full force to eliminate her.'

'Good! I will increase the reward on her head, and you hold up your end of the deal. Now get on it, Major General Smith!'

7

The winter of 1774, Virupatchi

THERE WAS A BUZZ OF ACTIVITY IN VIRUPATCHI. THE CONTINUED success of the ambushes seemed to have freshly boosted the morale of the men and women. Plans for the next rounds of attacks were laid out, and the soldiers were placing bets on who would capture the most loot and who would kill the most enemies. A collateral effect of the triumphs of the last couple of months was that many a fence-sitting chieftain started providing men and money to support the rani's cause.

Meanwhile, Vellachi fell into another bout of sickness and, on the advice of the doctors, was shifted from Virupatchi to a faraway village renowned for its medicines. Except for Vellachi's continued poor health, things were going according to plan and at a brisk pace.

The Maruthu brothers were on the field, discussing new tactics with soldiers. Gopal Nayakar was taking stock of the new supplies that had been captured. Thandavaraya Pillai and Rani Velu Nachiyar were in the main hall, calculating the next course of action and figuring out how to deal with the local chieftains.

A horseman frantically galloped onto the field towards Periya Maruthu Pandiyar.

'The English are coming! They are coming from the north!' he cried out.

The English rarely ventured deep into these forests. The scouts of Gopal Nayakar also hadn't noticed any large-scale movements by the English in the last few days. This sounded like a small detachment that clearly knew the path to their destination – Virupatchi. They had moved swiftly in the cover of darkness the previous night and early that morning to reach the edge of the citadel.

The older Maruthu didn't waste a moment. He ran to the end of the field, picked up a conch and blew it hard. All the men and women quickly rushed to the field.

He urgently addressed his people, 'The English have found our location. They are coming from the north. Arm yourself! Prepare for battle!'

Everybody got into a battle frenzy. Gopal Nayakar and Chinna Maruthu Pandiyar had already mounted their horses and begun directing the men into formation. Periya Maruthu Pandiyar's horse was taken to him, which he mounted, and thereafter shouted over to his brother, 'I will stall them with my Mandai dogs. Protect the queen!'

The older general then headed to the edge of the stables where his dogs were housed and ordered the stable boys to open the gates. This long-legged and slender breed of dogs covered in grey and brown coats of fur was feared for its viciousness, and now their master was about to unleash them on the English.

Having raised them, Periya Maruthu Pandiyar had trained

his Mandai dogs to hunt both man and beast. Today was their day to hunt the English.

The first line of English sepoys could be seen from the field to the north. With hills surrounding Virupatchi from three sides, the only way to the village was blocked by the English. They desperately wanted to finish off Velu Nachiyar and her army, leaving no exit options open. The solid mass of red-and-white infantry, shouldering their muskets, was moving in disciplined rhythm at a steady pace and in tight formation. They moved with strategy to get in range before firing their muskets.

The Sivaganga troops were still getting into formation.

Periya Maruthu Pandiyar, observing the movement of the English troops, thought to himself.

We will be in the firing range of the English muskets before we are ready. I need to do something to stall their army.

He cut through the agricultural fields on his horse, racing towards the English, with his Mandai dogs in tow.

As he got closer to the English, he gave a short and sharp command to his dogs, pointing towards the enemy army, 'Sic! Sic!'

The Mandai dogs dashed aggressively towards the infantry. Upon seeing the dogs, the frontline sepoys, who were getting ready to load their muskets, dropped their muskets and readied their swords. The sepoys behind them started fitting bayonets onto their muskets. But the dogs were fast and well-trained and went straight for the hamstrings and genitals of the soldiers.

A sizeable number of sepoys in the front line winced and collapsed as the dogs rabidly bit their nether regions. The sepoys were not dead, but seriously incapacitated, which rendered them unfit for further battle. The English army was brought to a halt, albeit temporarily. A few of the swifter sepoys were able to kill or maim the dogs with their swords, while the second line quickly came forward, taking out the remaining dogs with their bayonets. The loud barks of the dogs were quickly replaced by their wailing. The small English cavalry on the flanks broke ranks to assist the sepoys. The dogs were no match for the heavy hooves of the horses, and they were rapidly trampled by the English cavalry. Slowly and painfully, the squealing dogs were put to death.

But this attack gave enough time to the women of the Udaiyal army, dressed in maroon saris, to come ahead with their valaris. Just as the English thought they were finished with the dogs, there was a hail of valaris hurled at them by the women. The second line, which had come in front, bore the brunt of this attack. Their valaris slashed the sepoys' hands, legs and faces. A good many of them breathed their last. The remaining English troops moved back even as the Udaiyal women threw a second round of valaris. Getting themselves quickly out of range of the valaris, the English loaded their muskets and got into position. The muskets had a much longer range than the valaris. An English officer who was with the cavalry bellowed the order to fire.

The women didn't have appropriate armour, nor was there any place to seek shelter from the shots. As the firing began, the women retreated, running haphazardly, but the damage was catastrophic. Many brave Udaiyal soldiers bit the dust as they attempted to retreat. The sepoys continued with the musket fire until a handful of the women were out of range and the sepoys themselves were out of bullets.

After inflicting immense losses upon their opponents, the sepoys started marching forward. As they got closer to the open field, Chinna Maruthu Pandiyar gave the signal. From two directions, almost at flanking angles, the men who were behind the storehouses charged towards the English with aruvals in hand. At the same time, the young general and the chieftain led their respective cavalries from the stables to the rear of the smaller English cavalry which was right behind the infantry. A slugfest ensued on the field. The English swords clashed with the Sivaganga aruvals. In close combat, all metals were equal; the aruvals held their own against the English blades. The tables had turned, with the English now surrounded by the Sivaganga troops. The Sivaganga soldiers were slowly boxing in the English sepoys and their horses.

In the melee, about four English sepoys, armed with swords, managed to break through the cordon unnoticed and run towards Gopal Nayakar's house. They didn't need instructions from their officers, who were now pinned against the Sivaganga cavalry. They were on a mission – to take out Rani Velu Nachiyar – and they seemed to know her location beforehand. Perhaps spies had already clandestinely passed on valuable information about the rani's exact whereabouts to the English.

The main door of the house was not locked and the sepoys were able to barge inside with ease. There was nobody in the main hall.

The sepoy who got in first barked at the others, 'They must be somewhere here. Look around! I am not letting go of the reward!'

They split up, moving up the broad stairs of the large

house, and started searching one room at a time. There was nobody in any of the ones close to the main door. A couple of sepoys went towards Thandavaraya Pillai's quarters. On finding the door locked, they started kicking it down forcefully. The bolt holding the door closed couldn't take their blows and broke. The first sepoy went in only to have his throat slashed. Velu Nachiyar was standing inside with a sword that was now dripping with blood. The second sepoy came in with his sword in position. The queen stood guard in front of the prime minister, who too was armed. The sepoy's sword came down hard, but the rani blocked the blow with hers. She then pushed the sepoy away with all her might.

Hearing the commotion, the two remaining sepoys came into the room and blocked the entrance. Thandavaraya Pillai came over to stand next to Rani Velu with his own sword. An old man and a middle-aged woman were now standing opposite three battle-hardened soldiers. The sepoys knew the outcome of this unequal standoff. But before they could reach their foregone conclusion, one sepoy turned back in shock. He had been stabbed in the back with a kattari. In a split second, Periya Maruthu Pandiyar pulled the kattari out and stabbed it in the neck of the second sepoy. The third scrambled to attack him only to be put down by Velu Nachiyar's sword as he turned his back to the queen.

Even though all the sepoys in the house were killed, the queen and prime minister were not safe yet. Periya Maruthu Pandiyar moved the two out of the room and into the hallway further inside the house. Walking briskly in the hallway, he suddenly stopped. Stepping outside the carpeted area on the pathway, he lifted the carpet and opened a small wooden hatch on the floor underneath it.

'Please get inside. I will come back once we drive out the English.'

The rani complied and then, assisted by Periya Maruthu Pandiyar, helped the prime minister get inside as well. Periya Maruthu Pandiyar moved the carpet back to its original place. Stealing a dead sepoy's sword, he ran out of the house.

The cordon of the Sivaganga soldiers was broken, but the English officers seemed to have given an order of retreat to their army. The English soldiers were now going back in the direction they had come from. The Sivaganga soldiers were given orders to not chase them. The whole field was strewn with bodies; some barely alive, some long gone. The air was filled with dust, the stench of blood and the cries of the wounded. Thankfully, there had been no fires or serious damage to the structures. Periya Maruthu Pandiyar spotted his brother on his horse up north even as the English retreated. He walked all the way to see his brother.

Chinna Maruthu Pandiyar was ensuring no one pursued the English. He saw his elder brother and came forward to brief him, 'The English have retreated for now. But they will be back. This was not a full-fledged attack. They might be back with a bigger force. What are our losses?'

Looking at the bodies strewn behind him, Periya Maruthu Pandiyar said, 'We have taken some significant losses. But we still have a sizeable portion of our army still standing that is more than capable of sending those English bastards to hell.'

Chinna Maruthu Pandiyar looked at the dead bodies on the field as well. 'We are capable, but I am not sure if we can afford another huge loss of lives like today.'

That night, Velu Nachiyar spent time outside, assisting with the administration of medicines to the injured and observing the rituals being performed for burying the dead. Gopal Nayakar, the Maruthu brothers and Thandavaraya Pillai were by her side, helping her out.

The sheer number of fatalities and injured soldiers seemed to have taken a toll on the prime minister's spirits. Standing for a long time beside the queen, looking into the treatment of the injured, tired him out. He slowly walked to a bench near the storehouse and sat down. Finding an English musket lying on the ground, he picked it up and examined it closely. The workmanship involved in his bringing together metal and wood to create a powerful weapon was not lost on him.

A people that have the technology and resources to mass manufacture such barrels are not to be trifled with. We are fighting an unequal battle. No amount of our bravery can surmount the devastation these weapons cause. Our boys and girls will fall like cut grass every time we face them. I can't let this happen.

Thandavaraya Pillai was lost in thoughts and didn't realize that Velu Nachiyar was standing in front of him.

'Appa?'

His mind was immediately brought back to the scene in Virupatchi. He tried to stand up.

'My queen,' he laboured.

Velu Nachiyar held him back from standing and sat down next to him. They both looked at the Maruthu brothers, who were helping the men carry the fallen.

'I think the efforts of the Maruthu brothers are futile, my queen.'

A surprised rani asked, 'Why do think so, Appa?'

'We are fighting the English and their advanced weapons and tactics with our obsolete ones. We will not be able to stand up, let alone sustain our fight against them.'

Velu Nachiyar spoke with an undertone of anger, 'We are doing our best, Appa. People are giving everything, including their lives, to fight against the English!'

'Don't get me wrong, my queen. I did not mean to offend you or make light of today's sacrifices. I am merely saying that our supreme efforts are not sufficient in this asymmetrical warfare.'

'We have given everything to this fight – our body and soul. What more can we give?'

'We need to seek help, my queen. Sometimes even our best efforts are not enough. We need help. We will not be undermining the efforts and sacrifices made by our troops by asking for assistance. We need to chart a different course to reach our goal of taking back Sivaganga.'

The queen was flustered.

'What are you proposing? That we seek divine intervention? Perform magic? Wish the English away?'

'We should seek the assistance of supreme mortals, my queen. We need help from men who strike fear in the hearts of the English.'

'We don't make them fearful?'

'Man to man, we do strike fear. But how do we counter their muskets, their battle tactics and their monetary means? How I wish our bravery could overcome all of these shortcomings. But sadly, times are changing. The reality is that the things the English possess – better resources and technology – matter more than courage and valour today. We live in sad times indeed, my queen. But I am not one to lose hope. All I propose is that we seek help in overcoming these shortcomings.'

The weight of the deaths and wounds of the soldiers had negatively impacted the queen's state of mind. She felt agitated at what she construed as callous remarks by her prime minister. But a few minutes later, she journeyed back to the realm of calm. Her father figure had always put the interests of Sivaganga ahead of himself. He had always wished for the safety of their soldiers. He wouldn't suggest anything without keeping the interests of their troops in mind. Calmly, she prodded, 'Who will help us, Appa? You have informed us yourself that our allies aren't willing to commit fully to help us. Where else can we go?'

'There is one man the English fear the most. He is one of the rare few who has consistently defeated the English and is in position to affect an extinction of the English from these lands.'

'Who is this man?'

'Nawab Hyder Ali of Mysuru.'

The rani's soaring expectations sank just as quickly.

'The big rulers up north don't have time for kingdoms like ours,' she said. 'We are too small to get the nawab's attention. Why would he help us anyway?'

'The nawab of Mysuru and we have something in common – our hatred towards Arcot and the English. Now that alone may not be sufficient to sway him into helping us, but that shouldn't stop us from seeking his help. I don't think my health will permit me to make the journey north through Arcot territory to ask for his assistance. I could instead write a letter seeking his help in our war against the English.'

Before Velu Nachiyar could reply, the Maruthu brothers came over. Chinna Maruthu Pandiyar began anxiously, 'We need to move out of this place, my queen. The English know our position now. They are bound to come back with more forces. We need to set up another base, or we risk losing more people.'

'Yes, Chinna Pandi. We need to move out as soon as possible. Perform all the required rituals for the fallen before we retreat from our base. I would like you and Peri Pandi to scout for a new base at the earliest.'

Looking at Gopal Nayakar, who had joined the conversation after taking stock of the damages to the storehouse and the stables, she continued, 'I think Gopal could help us better if he separates himself from us and investigates our supplies. He will need to interact with the outside world to procure material for us.'

Nodding in agreement, the chieftain replied, 'As you wish, my queen. I will move closer to the towns and organize the logistics for you. I have enough safehouses at the edge of the forest that can accommodate me and a small contingent of men.'

Looking at her prime minister, Rani Velu Nachiyar continued, 'Appa, I would ask you to accompany Gopal. It would be easier for you to recoup your health in a safehouse than in the forest with us. Once you have recovered, you can join us. For now, I would like you to be in the safe hands of Gopal Nayakar.'

Surprisingly, the prime minister agreed without any resistance, 'Yes, my queen.'

He knew he would only weigh them down and be a liability

to their escape on account of his ill health. So, he gladly accepted his queen's order. This would also give him time in a proper place to write a letter to Nawab Hyder Ali asking for help and coordinate any follow-ups rather than being in the middle of a forest.

The following day, the first wave of men and supplies under Chinna Maruthu Pandiyar made their way out of Virupatchi into the forest, looking for a new base. Within the next few days, the entire army and supplies had moved out of Virupatchi leaving behind Gopal Nayakar and Thandavaraya Pillai with a few loyalists and retainers.

The latter managed to write a letter to Nawab Hyder Ali, but his ill health and the physical hardships of the last few months finally caught up with him and he passed away before he could dispatch the letter to Mysuru.

The winter of 1774, Fort St George in Madras

Major General Smith became a tad nervous after hearing about the English expedition in Virupatchi from Lieutenant Colonel Bonjour. Sitting in his musty-smelling office in Madras, he commanded, 'No more expeditions into hostile territory. Do you understand? We are not attracting the attention of Mysuru by stomping up and down their territory in pursuit of some reward given by Arcot!'

The statement was met with visible disappointment on Bonjour's face.

'Yes, sir,' he said plainly.

'Your action borders on insubordination. The last time, you got lucky. Your unprovoked action led us to capture Sivaganga with minimal loss of life. The council sided with you. But this time, we lost people for nothing, and we risk antagonizing Mysuru. Nobody will be on your side hereon, Lieutenant Colonel Bonjour.'

Bonjour knew the consequences of insubordination.

Execution.

'Yes, sir,' he repeated.

'How did you know that she was there?' the major general was curious to know.

'The spies of Arcot informed me of her location. There has been a steady stream of men and women going to Virupatchi. She is raising an army against us. Some of the chieftains in the Marava country informed us that she is seeking alliances with them. Also, you already knew that there has been an increase in the spate of attacks on our supply chain in Arcot and the neighbouring regions. We lost quite a few sepoys to these attacks. I wanted to act based on all the intelligence we have gathered and offer a befitting response to the hostile actions of the queen.'

'Yes, I am aware of the attacks. I thought it was the remnants of the Sivaganga army that were carrying out these attacks. They were low in intensity. This is expected and anticipated whenever we vanquish a kingdom. Their last vestiges will cause some problems after the majority has been eliminated. We must take care of them, and we will. Was your action proportionate to the problems they were causing? I don't think so. You marched a large contingent deep into the forest without anybody's knowledge, and you nearly decimated them. It looks like you were more interested in the large prize offered by Ameer-ul-Umara for Rani Velu Nachiyar's head than anything else. That's the only reason I can think of for you to initiate this attack.'

Lieutenant Colonel Bonjour kept his thoughts to himself.

I don't have a rebuttal for the Major General's assertion. After all, it is true that I was more interested in personal aggrandizement than anything else, and my action was purely in pursuit of the reward. But now, my life itself is on the line. Silence is my only defence against sure death.

In the absence of any response from Bonjour, Major General Smith continued, 'Your failure to take her out can have a cascading effect on us. News will now spread that the English troops were successfully resisted by a native queen. It is the sheer fear of the English that keeps many of these native princes in line and now, all thanks to you, we run a real risk of losing this aura. We need to re-establish the strength of the English in front of the natives. We need to salvage the pride of the English after this show of defiance by the queen. We can't let a native prince or a chieftain take us on and remain standing. The consequences of such a scenario are catastrophic. We will need to teach her a lesson and make an example out of her. At the same time, we can't take any actions that put us in direct conflict with the greater powers of the land. We need to assert ourselves against these smaller princes without getting into a battle with Mysuru.'

Bonjour finally broke his silence. 'Yes, sir. I understand the fragility of the situation. I would like a chance to get us out of this fix. If given the opportunity, I will ensure that the hegemony of the English is established again.'

'You were the one that caused this problem in the first place. You do realize that, don't you? Also, there is the question of trust. You seem to work more for your own selfish interests than the larger interests of the Company. Why should we risk our reputation by handing over this operation to you?'

The major general paused. His face changed from that of a stern taskmaster to a soft well-wisher's. Taking a deep breath, he continued gently, 'Abraham, don't fall for the lure of the reward given by the prince. Your loyalty should be towards the English and East India Company. You have a bright future if you work for the interests of the Company. So, don't pursue actions that jeopardize our interests. If you have a personal vendetta against the Sivaganga queen, pursue a more subtle approach. Send assassins to take her out. Get some turncoats from their side to do our work. But don't take drastic actions that can put our reputation at risk. You are also risking your career with these outlandish expeditions and the woeful execution of your plans. I am willing to give you the job as long as you toe the line of the Company. I will turn a blind eye to any amassment that you may undertake so long as the larger interests of the Company are safeguarded.'

'I understand the faults in my action. I will ensure that it never happens again. I thank you for the faith you still have in me. I will not let you down, sir,' Bonjour said earnestly.

'Good. Now, ensure that Rani Velu Nachiyar never steps into Arcot and other regions under our influence. Remember to take a subtle approach. It is a more arduous process, but it is safer, doesn't ruffle too many feathers and yet achieves the same result. Strengthen the supply lines with more soldiers or reduce movement on the risky routes. Stay out of Dindigul unless I tell you otherwise. If you want to work with Ameer-ul-Umara, get him to commit his men to any dirty work. Meanwhile, I will work with the chieftains to dissuade them from allying with Sivaganga. I will also warn the grain merchants against trading with the queen. I want her coerced into submission.'

'Yes, sir. I will pivot my actions. I will do as advised and take a more covert approach in getting rid of Rani Velu Nachiyar. My loyalty is and will always be towards the English.'

And this way I shall escape death by the skin of my teeth.

'Now go on and restore the pride of the English.'

8

Monsoon of 1778, somewhere deep in the Dindigul forests

'We need to shift our base, my queen. I just received intelligence from the nearby village that a large contingent of Arcot and English soldiers are on the prowl in this area. Someone must have leaked our location to them.'

'Again! Chinna Pandi, this is the fourth time we are changing our base. For the last five years, we have only been moving from one place to another.'

'I don't know how they locate us, my queen. Even though the residents of the villages nearby are loyal to us, there could be a couple of turncoats who disclose our whereabouts for money. Anyway, we are eliminating the English scouts that lurk in these forests. That should slow down the English considerably.'

'And yet they are able to track us time and again.'

'We are spending most of our time ameliorating our army rather than going after these traitors. We could spend more time and effort tracing these double-crossers, but I would recommend that we focus that time on building the strength of our troops.'

Right that moment, Kuyili entered the tent. As the rani's adopted daughter, she didn't need permission or a summons to visit the queen. Meanwhile, Vellachi, the queen's biological daughter, continued to stay away from her mother, well hidden in a village of loyalists and away from the prying eyes of the English and Arcot. Her chronic health condition would not have allowed her to survive the arduous forest life.

Velu Nachiyar saw her daughter in Kuyili, and the teenaged girl was now trained in martial arts just as Vellachi would have been had she been healthy.

Kuyili stood next to the queen, who was seated on the edge of her chair across the tent, while Chinna Maruthu Pandiyar stood at the entrance. She listened in silence.

The queen was not convinced by Chinna Maruthu Pandiyar's hypothesis.

'What if the traitor is amongst us, Chinna Pandi? We might have a few turncoats in every village. But some of our previous camps were nowhere near a village. How could anyone have seen us or known about our whereabouts then?

The general remained quiet. He kept his head down. The queen immediately understood the shift in his body language.

'Chinna Pandi, I know that you and Peri Pandi have brought every person here. You would personally vouch for all of them. I do not have a shred of doubt in your or Peri Pandi's loyalty and capability. But people change. The lure of money and fortune can sway many a weak-hearted man. Look around us; all that we can offer our people is pain and hardship. These harsh conditions can break a man. So, it's quite plausible that one amongst us could have succumbed to the allure of riches offered by the prince of Arcot. Maybe we should spend some time scrutinizing the members in our fold.'

'Sure, my queen. But we have a more immediate concern right now. It is not safe here anymore. We should move further inside the forest.'

'And at what cost are we securing our safety?'

'The deeper we get into the forest, the further away we are from Sivaganga. It will be more difficult for us to recruit additional troops now. We need to stay close to Sivaganga to inspire more to join us. But for the sake of your safety, we need to move farther from our home. Once we have enough men and women, we can shift back closer to Sivaganga.'

'How can we then scale our recruitment if we keep moving further and further from Sivaganga? We were driven out of the Padamathur fort and then the Manamadurai fort. Now, we don't even reside in a fort. We have never gone beyond the numbers we had at Virupatchi.'

'We are trying our best, my queen. But for now, your safety is paramount.'

'I am not blaming you, Chinna Pandi. I am merely expressing my frustration at not being any closer to reclaiming Sivaganga than we were five years ago. We are always on the back foot, with no opportunity to take a step forward. I could not even offer my last respects to Appa. The English and Arcot nawab have kept us on our toes and now have us here – holed up in this forest,' the queen said dismally.

The general didn't reply; he simply mirrored the queen's dismay.

The pond around their current location, brimming in the monsoon, was a source of water for the followers of Velu Nachiyar. Moving the base from here was going to be a step down. It would be extremely hard to find a similar source of water elsewhere in the forest on the borders of Arcot. But it was exigent to move away from this place. Rani Velu Nachiyar reluctantly acquiesced to Chinna Maruthu Pandiyar's request. Their choice of a base was deteriorating each time they changed locations. Nobody expected to be in a better place after moving out from here.

The resourceful Maruthu general had already found another location to set up the base. The present camp was being winded down through the night. Despite their lack of sleep, all the soldiers and camp followers began their journey to the next camp at the break of dawn. The walk was now through lush green forests. Unlike the hot summer, this season offered the luxury of shade, but the ground ran slushy due to rain, which made the walk a lot more arduous.

The group finally reached the camp site by late evening. Periya Maruthu Pandiyar was in charge of setting up camp, and he made sure everyone put in work before resting.

'There is no rest until the setting up is done. I don't want to see anyone idle. We will have dinner only after the tents have been put up.'

With the elder Maruthu Pandiyar's aggressive prodding, the camp was set up, and dinner was served late in the night inside the camp grounds. Everyone was exhausted, and they soon drifted off to sleep.

The moon had risen in the clear sky. Except for the sound of critters, it was relatively quiet. Velu Nachiyar woke up with a start.

Something is wrong!

She got up, wrapped herself in a shawl and stepped out of her tent.

Kuyili had a rope around the neck of Vetrivel, the silambam trainer, trying her hardest to strangle the burly man. Short and petite, Kuyili, who was half his height, had climbed over his back and was now holding the rope tightly to choke the trainer's windpipe. The big man was trying hard to throw Kuyili off like a rag doll but she just wouldn't give in.

Vetrivel was staggering to his left and right but didn't lose his balance. He kept trying to pull Kuyili's leg with one hand and trying to break the chokehold with the other. He was clearly losing the battle on both the fronts.

A shocked Rani Velu Nachiyar shouted, 'Kuyili!'

Hearing the queen's voice, everyone nearby rushed out of their tents. By then, Vetrivel was on his knees, and Kuyili was pulling the rope harder than ever. Everyone stood stunned for a moment. The man finally lost his breath and collapsed. A soldier came over and pulled Kuyili away.

The girl was still breathing heavily, aggression writ large on her face. She didn't resist the man who pulled her away. Another man came over to the trainer and examined him.

'He is dead,' the man declared.

Looking at the queen, Kuyili began, 'He is the traitor! I saw him go out in the dusk and come back now. He is the traitor, Amma!'

The queen looked at Kuyili, flustered. She wouldn't give up. Ordering the soldiers, she announced, 'Search him! Search his belongings!'

Without seeking permission from the queen, the man near the dead trainer searched through Vetrivel's clothes. At the same time, another started rummaging through his personal belongings in his tent.

Both the men returned to the queen with multiple small pouches filled with gold pagodas and a small, rectangular brown leather bag. The queen felt the texture of the pouch cloth and then proceeded to open the leather bag. There was a letter inside it. After perusing the letter, she looked up and called out, 'Kuyili, come over here!'

The man holding Kuyili released her. She walked over to the queen, who still stood a few inches taller than her. As Kuyili came closer, the rani pulled her to her bosom and kissed her forehead.

'You are making a habit of saving your old mother, child,' she said tenderly.

Looking up at her mother, Kuyili smiled broadly. There was innocence in her eyes. Her smile made her look like a little girl again. No one could believe, looking at her now, that this girl killed a martial artist twice her size with her bare hands.

Still holding on to Kuyili with one arm, Velu Nachiyar announced, 'This letter is from Mallari Rayan, a known English loyalist who now resides in Sivaganga. Vetrivel received gold in these pouches every time he disclosed our location to him. He was the spy who lived amongst us and caused us so much hardship. But it's all over now, for Vetrivel has been killed. I don't think the English will be able to locate us with ease from here on. This girl here has protected us from the nefarious designs of the English and the nawab of Arcot.' The queen felt and beamed like a proud mother.

There was a spontaneous cheer for the young girl. The sixteen-year-old had a broad smile that spread ear to ear as everyone chanted her name. She was not intimidated by all this attention. There was tinge of innocence in her eyes as people continued to chant her name. It was almost as if she didn't realize the gravity of her actions.

Holding her adopted daughter in a motherly embrace, the queen declared, 'From here on, Kuyili will be my chief bodyguard.'

The announcement was followed by a great acclamation from everyone. They were clearly elated with the decision.

Once the cheers died down, Velu Nachiyar continued, 'As my chief bodyguard, Kuyili will now be the leader of our revered Udaiyal army.'

The announcement was followed by even louder exhilaration. Amidst all this shouting, Kuyili kept smiling in the warm embrace of her mother, not realizing the magnitude of the honour bestowed on her.

'I am just happy that Amma is safe. I will always protect her, whether I am her bodyguard or not. My happiness lies in my mother's happiness. Her unabated love is all that I seek,' Kuyili responded softly.

Later that night, Chinna Maruthu Pandiyar was summoned into the queen's tent. On seeing him, she said, 'I am not sure if our present location has already been disclosed to Arcot and the English by that traitor. He could also be working with others. For the sake of precaution, we must send out scouts tomorrow to see if there is any enemy activity in the vicinity. We need to be prepared to move again if the need arises, Chinna Pandi.'

'As you command, my queen. I will coordinate with Peri Pandi if we need to move again and keep you informed.'

Thank you, Chinna Pandi.'

There was an audible sign of resignation in the general's voice.

'Your spirits seem low, Chinna Pandi. What worries you? Our army is stronger than ever. We cannot be vanquished, come what may.'

'Yes, my queen. But our goal is to take back our beloved Sivaganga, and even after so many years, we are only running away from her enemies. Just as you mentioned the other day, we haven't taken a single step forward in the pursuit of our goal.'

He paused for a moment. Standing up, he continued talking passionately, 'Please order us, my queen. We will march right away to Sivaganga. There isn't a man worth his salt in the ranks of the English at Sivaganga who can defeat us. Let us stop this play of hide-and-seek and face them head-on.'

Smiling at her general, the queen replied, 'We will, Chinna Pandi, in due course of time.' She didn't voice her thoughts for fear of dampening the younger Maruthu Pandiyar's spirits further.

Our army's ranks will thin out completely before we can reach the gates of Sivaganga. Even the soldiers on the prowl outnumber our army vastly. Going head-on against our enemies who are also equipped with advanced weaponry will be suicidal. As a queen responsible for the safety and well-being of my people, I won't put them in harm's way despite my generals' fighting spirit.

'When will that time come, my queen?'

He still believes our bravery can trump the clear disadvantage we have in terms of money, men and arms. I can't dishearten Chinna Pandi. I can't let his morale suffer.

'We need more brave men like you, Chinna Pandi,' the queen responded, in hopes of motivating him. 'We need to recruit more people. You are doing a good job getting more men and women into our fold. Keep continuing with the recruitment. I promise you that the time will come soon when we take back our home. For now, get some rest. Let me know if we need to move our base. I will retire as well.'

'Yes, my queen.'

Bowing to his queen, Chinna Maruthu Pandiyar exited the tent and retired to his own. Velu Nachiyar sat silently as the torches outside her tent continued to burn, bringing some light into the tent.

I can't go on like this forever. I can't stake the future of my people in this futile game with the English. I need to take drastic measures to change this status quo. But what can I do?

The silence hung heavy in the tent. The rani was feeling helpless and yet she couldn't express it to anyone.

Even after so many years, we are still hiding in the forests. I am powerless against my enemies. I have nothing to give in return for the faith placed in me. I feel helpless. How I wish my husband was here. I wish I was safe in his arms. I am all alone now.

Even though her eyes welled up, Velu Nachiyar didn't let her tears win.

I can't let the death of my husband go in vain. But what can I do? I have nobody to turn to. Appa too passed away, leaving me with no guidance. He would have shown me a way forward.

Suddenly, the thought of her Appa struck something in her.

I should seek the assistance of Nawab Hyder Ali, just as Appa had suggested. I wonder why we never got a response – perhaps because the nawab's messengers could never locate us in our years of moving around. I can't wait for his reply any longer. These are drastic times, and I need to take extreme measures. This is my only option. I need to make this count.

There was a never-before-seen zeal in the queen's eyes. She had made up her mind. She went to sleep determined to put her plan into action the following day.

The Maruthu brothers were called for a meeting with the queen the next morning.

'I have called you here to inform you about a decision that I made last night. I will make a journey to meet Nawab Hyder Ali at his capital, Srirangapatna. I will request his assistance in reclaiming Sivaganga—'

Periya Maruthu Pandiyar interrupted, 'I am coming with you, my queen.'

His younger brother followed close on his heels, 'We trust your decision and want to be with you to protect you, my queen.'

Refusing the offer made by the Maruthu brothers, the queen continued, 'You have a bigger responsibility here. I want both of you to protect the troops and the camp followers until I return. I will take two diplomats who can double up as my retainers. This is, after all, a envoys mission.'

'But, my queen, the journey is fraught with risks. Your life would be under constant threat. It's our duty to protect you. We will come with you.'

Velu Nachiyar replied in a firm voice, 'This is the order of the queen of Sivaganga! You will do as I say!'

Periya Maruthu Pandiyar remained silent for a moment, but he couldn't hold himself back. He retaliated with fervour and remorse, 'That's what our king said as well before we lost him. I am not going to lose you – not on my watch. I insist we come with you! Please, my queen.'

Rani Velu Nachiyar was lost for words.

They still blame themselves for the death of my husband. I can't let them carry this guilt. I need to give in to their wish, but I also need them to protect the army. I must find a middle ground.

'Alright, you can both come along but you will be with me only till I cross Arcot. Once we are past hostile territory, it will be safe to traverse the Mysuru kingdom to its capital. After we cross Arcot, promise me that you will return to protect the troops and keep them away from the English. You need to have faith in me and my decision. I know I will be safe in Mysuru, and I promise to return with good news.'

Periya Maruthu Pandiyar was still not convinced. He was about to protest, but Chinna Maruthu Pandiyar held him back.

'We only wish for your safety, my queen,' the younger Maruthu general said. 'At the same time, we have the utmost faith in your decision. We will guard you until you are in the safe environs of Mysuru.'

'Thank you, Chinna Pandi. Please take care of Vellachi too, while I am not here. Take Kuyili under your wing. Train her in the arts of a soldier. Make me proud.'

'Yes, my queen,' they spoke in unison, bowing their heads.

That same morning, Velu Nachiyar, along with the Maruthu brothers and two diplomats, separated from the larger group at the camp and started towards Srirangapatna on horseback. All of them were disguised as traders, even the rani, who was dressed up as a male trader. Their objective was to reach the capital of Mysuru without attracting any attention.

The journey was anything but monotonous, with a lot of streams to cross as a result of the monsoons, trails vanishing under thickets of grass and the surrounding wild animals. The abundance of food and water on the trail was offset by the humidity and the menace of critters. But all of this was of no concern to the travelling party, for their biggest concern was to cross enemy territory without being detected. After two days of travel, they finally entered Arcot.

The group had dismounted their horses and were now resting next to a rivulet. The sun was high up in the sky, but the travellers were protected from its harsh rays by the thick foliage all around them. Periya Maruthu Pandiyar was playing with the two Mandai dogs that he had brought along. Chinna Maruthu Pandiyar was rearranging the sacks on the horses to even out the load. The two diplomats were dozing under the cool shade of the trees. Rani Velu Nachiyar was gazing at the fast-moving stream, reminiscing about happier times with her husband, as she sat with her back to a tree. Everything was serene and relaxed.

All of a sudden, the Mandai dogs started barking in a particular direction inside the forest. Everyone grew alert and stood up, looking in the same direction. Four sepoys, dressed in ragged red shirts and torn white pants, emerged from the wilderness to face the group. They were surprised to see five traders in the middle of the forest.

The oldest of the sepoys, flaunting an unshaven beard and grey whiskers, shouted gruffly, 'Hey! Who are you? What are you doing here?'

One of the diplomats bowed to the soldiers. 'We are textile traders headed to Arcot to procure cloth material from the merchants there.'

'Why are you travelling through the forest like this? There is a proper road to Arcot. Why aren't you taking that? And your turbans look familiar. You are coming from Sivaganga, aren't you?'

The second diplomat answered the question.

'We are from Sivaganga. We took this route because we had to visit merchants in Dindigul. This was the shortest route from there to Arcot. We just wanted to save time.'

The sepoys went back a few metres, out of earshot, and started murmuring amongst themselves. After a few moments, the old sepoy came back to address the travelling band.

'It is dangerous to travel in these regions. There are bandits swarming all over the place who will murder you for the money that you are carrying. You will need protection.'

The diplomat, looking at the physically advantaged Maruthu brothers, said, 'I think we are well covered to handle bandits. Thank you for your concern.'

The answer didn't seem to go down well with the sepoys.

'The bandits outnumber you ten to one. They will kill you and relieve you of all your gold and silver.'

The diplomat smiled and replied, 'We are not carrying much gold with us. We are carrying letters of credit. They are of no use without our bearing them personally. If we are killed, the letters become useless. We have nothing that could attract the attention of the bandits.'

There was visible anger on the sepoys' faces.

'You are carrying no money?'

The soldiers started fidgeting with their swords. Periya Maruthu Pandiyar clenched the kattari that was hidden under his vest. There was palpable tension in the air. Before things could take a turn for the worse, Velu Nachiyar discreetly took out a small pouch hidden in the folds of her clothes, handed it over to the diplomat and signalled at him to hand it over to the sepoys.

The diplomat diligently handed the pouch over to the sepoys while saying, 'Please accept this gold on our behalf. We seek your protection as we navigate the forests.'

The oldest sepoy snatched the pouch from him and looked into its contents. He went back to the others who were standing behind him. The four soldiers huddled together and split the gold amongst themselves.

The old sepoy then came back with a big smile on his face.

'You are under our protection now. We patrol these areas. You can travel through the forest without fear. We will ensure that you encounter no bandits. Good day.'

With a quick goodbye, the sepoys vanished in the direction they had come from.

Velu Nachiyar waited for the sepoys to go out of earshot before speaking, 'I think we bought ourselves free passage for a couple more days. Let's make good use of it and cross the Arcot territory.'

Everyone got back on their horses and continued onward. Due to their chance encounter with the English, there was a sense of urgency that engulfed them all to cross over to Mysuru. In a day and a half, the group managed to reach the frontiers of Mysuru. It was time to split into two groups – one was to proceed further and the other would say goodbye and return.

Periya Maruthu Pandiyar was still concerned about the safety of his queen.

'We will come along with you if you change your mind, my queen,' he offered.

'We are in safer environs now, Peri Pandi. We will continue on our own, as originally planned. I am concerned about the safety of your trip back. Please lie low and out of trouble. Your leadership is paramount for our people.'

'We will always be safe with your blessings, my queen.'

Blessing the two, the rani and her two diplomats continued onwards to Srirangapatna while the Maruthu brothers traced their path back to camp to uphold their promise of training Kuyili, taking care of Vellachi and protecting the troops.

The terrain changed as the queen-led group moved north. More and more hills started obstructing their path. In the absence of good scouts, they ended up spending additional time locating passes to cross the hills, thus delaying their progress.

Velu Nachiyar proposed, 'All we need to do is find the river Kaveri. We can then follow it right up to Srirangapatna. It is, after all, a large island on the river.'

The other diplomat concurred with the queen, 'I would propose we climb hills to locate the river.'

Rani Velu Nachiyar agreed with the proposal. Even as the group sought passage through the hills, they also scaled them every day of their journey to locate the river. After a few days, the three were finally able to locate the river Kaveri and, along with it, a path through the hills, following which, they made their way past them. The terrain now turned flat, and civilization started making an appearance again. They quickly got on the road leading to the capital of the Mysuru kingdom.

With the capital getting closer, they started discussing their plan of action.

'I don't think you should reveal yourself, my queen. We don't know the intentions of Nawab Hyder Ali yet. We need to play it safe when we get an audience with him,' one of the diplomats suggested.

'Also, we never know who we may encounter there. Spies of the English and Arcot are bound to be in the area. We need to be wary of that as well. If you reveal yourself, that carries a significant risk. We would like to do the talking with your guidance for now and seek the nawab's assistance,' the other diplomat said.

The queen agreed to follow her diplomats' proposal.

'Alright,' she said. 'I will continue being in disguise. This way I will not attract much attention.'

'When we seek assistance from the nawab, what can we offer in return?' one of the diplomats asked.

The queen replied, 'We will leverage his hatred for the English and Arcot to support us. We will need to position ourselves as useful allies for him to beat his opponents. He may see us as pawns in a larger political game. We should make ourselves seen as as such. In return, his help would help us take back Sivaganga.'

'What specific assistance are we asking him for?'

'We would need military, monetary and diplomatic aid. Mere moral support would do us no good. We need to get something concrete out of him—'

The rani stopped midway. She was looking at the capital of Mysuru that was visible on the horizon. The island was much bigger than her expectations. The river looked like a moat around the island. Eyen more imposing were the thick, high walls that encircled it.

So, the legend is true. It is impossible to capture Srirangapatna.

Velu Nachiyar instructed her diplomats, 'Get our letters of credence ready; we will need them to enter the capital.'

9

Post-monsoon of 1778, Srirangapatna

IT HAD BEEN A WEEK IN THE CAPITAL OF MYSURU, SRIRANGAPATNA, and Nawab Hyder Ali was yet to give an audience to the guests from Sivaganga. Rani Velu Nachiyar, still in disguise as a male trader, explored the capital with her two diplomats. The queen was enamoured by the sights and sounds of the city. It was always buzzing with people from all around the world practising their trade, selling their wares and working under the famed administration of Mysuru. English and French merchants rubbed shoulders with Marwari traders from the north. The markets were filled with items sourced from everywhere. Intricate clocks from England were placed right next to spices from the Malabar region. Trade and commerce seemed to be the beating heart of the city.

Despite being protected by the Kaveri river on all sides, a moat had been dug around the fort to make it even more inaccessible for enemies and attackers. The tall gopura of the Ranganatha Swamy temple was visible from all points of the fortified city. The temple shared space with the impressive Jamia Masjid, with its unblemished cream walls, and the churches of French Jacobins within the walls of the fort. The place was practically impregnable, and the sheer wealth of the city astounded the queen. There was no dearth of food or water here.

Several French officers who were part of the Mysuru army were training their soldiers in European military tactics on the barrack grounds. As for the beasts in battle, they had at their disposal war elephants, innumerable horses and even Rajput camel artillery.

Ten days after entering Srirangapatna, it was finally the rani's turn to receive an audience with the nawab in his durbar. Hyder Ali had kept a day aside for meeting the diplomats who had arrived in the capital. Velu Nachiyar was one of many. She remained in disguise, fearing assassination attempts by the agents of Arcot and the English in Srirangapatna.

The durbar was spread over two levels, with all the diplomats in attendance on the ground floor. The first level was, for all practical purposes, out of bounds for outsiders. There was a small balcony on the first floor that projected forward. This is where the nawab sat to address the people downstairs. To the left of this balcony was the zenana, from where the royal ladies could listen in on the proceedings of the durbar. The section was covered with intricately designed wooden *jaalis*. The section to the right was completely covered and housed the personal quarters for the nawab and his confidants.

On the ground floor, the diplomats were given designated spots to stand in with the more important ones, like the

Marathas, the French and the nizam of Hyderabad in front, and those from comparatively smaller and less powerful kingdoms behind. Rani Velu Nachiyar stood almost at the rear of this bevy with her diplomats. Nawab Hyder Ali had still not come into the durbar.

One of the rani's diplomats grew concerned. 'There are so many people here. Do you think we will be able to meet the nawab today?'

Velu Nachiyar looked at the diplomat, a little perplexed by his question.

The rigours of continuous guerrilla warfare have taken a toll on my young diplomats. They lack exposure to the workings of great powers, and their inexperience shows in their worries. I need to guide them and assuage their concerns.

She calmly replied, 'I have heard stories about the nawab and his intense work ethic. He just doesn't stop. Also, his mind remains sharp despite the workload. Let's hope for the best.'

A few minutes later, the court usher announced the entrance of Hyder Ali.

He seemed to have the features of a soldier rather than those of an aristocrat or a king. He was well-built, his face sunburnt and wizened. It was clear that age had not been his friend. He wore a simple white garb with no ornaments. His yellow turban had just one jewelled brooch to hold it together. The sword in his hand, far from being bejewelled, seemed to have witnessed a lot of action, with both scabbard and hilt showing signs of wear and tear. His look conveyed that he would have been more at home at a general's headquarters than at the durbar of a nawab.

Hyder Ali didn't wait for any pleasantries and quickly got to the task at hand. Diplomats stepped forward, presented their credentials and put forward their requests to the nawab. He then dictated his replies and counter-proposals on the spot to his writers sitting on the floor below. The nawab conversed with the diplomats in a variety of languages, ranging from Persian, Urdu and Kannada to Telugu and Marathi. He knew a smattering of English and French as well. Occasionally, he caught some diplomats off guard with his pointed questions. This exercise went on for a few hours with Hyder Ali showing no sign of fatigue; he was sharp as ever. Diplomats were being dispatched with solutions or replies at a good pace. Then it was the turn of governors and rulers of smaller kingdoms to apprise him of the situation in their provinces. The nawab was seamlessly shifting from topics related to the treasury and economy to those of military and intelligence reports. He had a complete grip on all matters. Finally, the usher announced the names of the diplomats of Sivaganga.

The senior diplomat came forward to address the nawab. 'Your highness, we are diplomats from the kingdom of Sivaganga. Our lands have been illegally taken over by the English and Arcot. We are here to seek your assistance to restore the rightful rulers of Sivaganga and undo the wrong that has been committed against them—'

The nawab stopped him midway.

'Look around you. Kings and governors themselves have come here in person to seek my assistance. If Sivaganga needs assistance, then its king must come here in person to ask for help.'

Before the situation could unravel, Rani Velu Nachiyar came

forward and removed her turban, letting her long hair cascade out. She spoke in elegant Kannada: 'It is my misfortune that I, Rani Velu Nachiyar, the queen of Sivaganga, have to travel undercover to even seek your help.'

Nawab Hyder Ali looked stunned for a moment. He was astonished to see that this woman from a country situated in the deep south could speak such chaste Kannada and that she had managed to enter his durbar incognito. Of course, his security detail would be reprimanded for letting this happen, but he was impressed by her nevertheless.

'Go ahead,' the nawab ordered, smiling.

'With deceit and treachery, the prince of Arcot and the English murdered my husband, the king of Sivaganga, Muthuvaduganatha Thevar. They murdered innocent women and children in our towns and villages. They have taken over our beloved Sivaganga and forced me and my followers out of our palace. We have been hiding in the depths of the forests for the last six years. We have still not given up and are trying to raise an army to fight against them despite our limited resources. But with thinning means, money and arms, our hope of regaining our kingdom is dwindling. There is only one man my enemies fear and that, your highness, is the nawab of Mysuru, Hyder Ali Khan. I seek the assistance of the mortal enemy of the English and Arcot in overthrowing them and restoring the right order in Sivaganga. I seek assistance from my elder brother, my *anna*, to right the wrong that has been done to his *thangi*, his little sister.'

Nawab Hyder Ali listened to her patiently. He was clearly impressed by her passion and courage to make the perilous journey to Srirangapatna.

I hear your call for assistance. Please give me some time to make my decision. Until then, I request you to stay here as a state guest of Mysuru.'

Rani Velu Nachiyar and her diplomats bowed to the nawab and were politely ushered out of the durbar. They proceeded to the guest quarters inside a large palace specifically built for the state guests of Mysuru. The rani and her entourage now patiently waited to hear from the nawab.

A week later, Hyder Ali was in his private hall late at night with his general Purnaiah, who was apprising him of the situation south of the Madras Presidency.

'The only risk we would face on our march to Madras is from Arcot, my lord,' Purnaiah said. 'As long as our troops maintain good speed in their movements, the danger from Arcot would be negligible. But if we were to get bogged down anywhere in the middle, we run the risk of getting cut off from our southern forts.'

'Wallajah will run to Madras the minute I step out of my fort,' Hyder Ali replied. 'All his forts will be thinly garrisoned. I will run over everything that belongs to him between Mysuru and Madras. What about the English in Thanjavur who are further south?'

'The English are more focused on the supply lines, especially food, from Thanjavur to Madras. They are also providing protection to the Thanjavur Marathas there. My assessment is that they would be more focused on protecting their supply lines than attacking us.'

'But if things go bad for the English, we run a risk of them moving up?

'That's a possibility, my lord.'

'Well, we have to pin them down there before I deal with the English at Madras. What about the situation in Sivaganga? The English have a garrison there as well. The queen of Sivaganga is here seeking our help.'

'Sivaganga is the smaller Marava kingdom, which is relatively close to our Dindigul province. Having an ally there would be very useful. We reduce the risk of attacks on our southern frontier and, when you decide to attack the English further south, in Madras, we could secure them as loyalists who could aid us. Also, the probability of any unpleasant surprises during our expedition would be greatly reduced if we have the people of Sivaganga on our side.'

'How do you propose we help them, Purnaiah?'

'Money and men should be sufficient, my lord. We can help them mount an attack and restore the queen back on her throne at Sivaganga. Our intelligence reports say that the English have a garrison in the Sivaganga fort, which shouldn't pose much of a challenge to our troops.'

The nawab considered this for a moment. 'How much money and men would be required?' he asked.

'We don't need to earmark money and men separately for the queen, my lord. We can relieve Sivaganga when we undertake our campaign against the English in the south.'

'I had sent over some spies to Sivaganga after my meeting with the queen. The English have stored a lot of ammunition in Sivaganga, but the garrison is relatively small. If we plan a move on Sivaganga just before our main expedition, we could ensure that we take a lot of ammunition off the hands of the English that could potentially be used against us when we march to Madras, thus making our lives easier during the main expedition.'

'In that case, we need to make our move at the earliest, my lord.'

'What is your opinion about our commander at Dindigul, Syed Karki?'

'Syed Karki hasn't made a wrong move until now. He has had quite a bit of success on the battlefield as well. Deploying him to drive out the English from Sivaganga would be a very prudent move.'

'The boy is certainly ambitious. He might be a bit down about not being part of the main campaign against the English. Nevertheless, the Sivaganga operation would be a good opportunity for him.'

'Yes, my lord. Do you want to undertake this operation independently of the queen?'

'Absolutely not! I want Syed Karki to work with the queen. It will be a win-win situation. I have seen very few people with the passion and fire that I saw in the queen's eyes that day. My spies have informed me that she has been waging guerrilla warfare against the English and Arcot for almost six years now since the death of her husband. She has managed to not only survive but also be a thorn in the side of the English for this long with her limited means and small army. So, I am sure her troops will have the same zeal as their queen. Working together would definitely make the job easier. More importantly, I would then have a strong ally down south. Syed Karki could also use some learning from her.'

'We will need to drive out a lot of Arcot and English soldiers from the other towns within Sivaganga before we mount an attack on the main fort itself.'

'I will leave the operational details to Syed Karki, Purnaiah. He needs to get the Sivaganga kingdom back to the queen.'

'I beg your pardon, my lord. I am sure you have done your due diligence. But can we really trust the queen's intentions? How can we be sure that she is not playing us against our enemies?'

'Purnaiah, I have survived this treacherous world for so long only by relying on my instincts. And my instincts tell me to trust Rani Velu Nachiyar. That doesn't mean I am placing my trust in her blindly. Like you say, I have done my due diligence in analyzing the pros and cons of my decision. I have considered the outcomes of helping her and denying her. I have also looked at the magnitude of help we can offer her. We have a great deal to gain and little to lose by offering her help. Let's face it – the queen is all alone, with the English and the Arcot prince baying for her blood. She wouldn't want to antagonize another power. In fact, I think she will be grateful once we help her get back her kingdom.'

Purnaiah nodded, satisfied with the nawab's arguments.

Hyder Ali continued, 'Work with our intelligence and Syed Karki to make an assessment of the resources required. Let them utilize the troops at Dindigul. Work with our treasury to ascertain how much we can afford to shell out for this operation. If we need to transport gold to Dindigul for this operation, make it happen. Let's help the queen of Sivaganga reclaim her throne. After all, that's the least an elder brother can do for his sister.'

'Yes, my lord,' a smiling Purnaiah replied.

A few days later, a courtier entered the quarters of Velu Nachiyar at the state guest house.

'You have been granted a private audience with the nawab of Mysuru, your highness. He requests your presence tomorrow afternoon at the durbar, two hours before the reception.'

The rani, having anxiously waited all this while for some good news, was filled with renewed hope on hearing the courtier's message.

'Please convey my gratitude to the nawab for granting us an audience. I will be present at the prescribed time.'

Velu Nachiyar arrived at the durbar at the appointed hour. The place seemed to have a different ambience compared to the last time, with only the court writers, courtiers and soldiers in attendance.

A courtier came over to her. 'Your presence is awaited at the royal quarters upstairs, your highness.'

She was escorted upstairs to a wide, well-carpeted room with a low ceiling. Hyder Ali was sitting on his masand with Purnaiah standing by his side.

Purnaiah welcomed the queen, 'Thank you for coming here, your highness.'

Rani Velu Nachiyar thanked them for inviting her.

With the niceties over, Hyder Ali began, 'Taking stock of the situation, I realized that helping a rightful queen such as yourself reclaim the throne of Sivaganga is a noble act. The Almighty himself would bless the man who avenges the wrongs done to you. It would be a grave injustice to not help my sister in this hour of need. Rani Velu Nachiyar, I have decided to aid you in your fight against the deceitful English and the treacherous prince of Arcot. I will help you regain Sivaganga and reinstate you on the throne as the deserved and just queen of your kingdom.'

The queen's eyes welled up, but she held back her tears. Blinking them away, a smile broke out on her face.

'Thank you, your highness,' she said in a voice teeming with gratitude. 'I am indebted to you for life.' Velu Nachiyar bowed her head, and there was a slight shiver in her body.

'I am merely doing the right thing,' the nawab replied. 'I look forward to us forging a strong relationship between Mysuru and Sivaganga as we drive out our enemies.'

'Yes, your highness. Sivaganga will never forget its friends. I promise you Sivaganga will stand you through thick and thin just like Mysuru has stood by us today in this hour of despair.'

'Thank you, thangi. My help is not mere words. I am backing them with 5,000 of the finest infantrymen of the Mysuru army and 5,000 cavalrymen from the famed Kuzzaks – the best light cavalry in the land. I will also be issuing 400 pagodas every month to you to sustain your army and your operations until Sivaganga is recaptured. Purnaiah will fill you in with more details before you leave Srirangapatna.'

'Thank you, your highness.' A single tear dropped down her face as Velu Nachiyar smiled with grace in acknowledgement.

A courtier came in and guided the queen out of the room and the durbar. She was taken to Purnaiah's office.

'The general will be joining you shortly, your highness,' the courtier said and took his leave.

Rani Velu Nachiyar was alone in a large, well-furnished office.

Things will finally turn for the better now. Our six years of exile will finally come to an end. All the pain and suffering will have been worth it.

In a few minutes, Purnaiah came into his office.

'Apologies for keeping you waiting, your highness. I was finalizing the finer details of the help offered to you by the nawab of Mysuru.'

Velu Nachiyar waited for Purnaiah to brief her.

'We would like you to proceed to the fort of Dindigul to meet with our commander there, Syed Karki. We will give you the letters of support that you will need to present to him, after which he will provide you with the men and horses promised by the nawab. The cost of the upkeep of the troops supplied by us will be borne by Mysuru. In addition to this, Syed Karki will also send you with the 400 pagodas every month for sustaining your operations as promised by the nawab.

'The troops would be under your overall command, with Syed Karki as your military advisor. In case of any disagreement, I request you bring it to my attention at the earliest. We are wishing for a successful operation as much as you, and we don't want any wrangles on this journey.'

'Thank you, General Purnaiah. I am sure there will be no scope for any divergences in our goal.'

'I pray for the same, your highness. Syed Karki has been informed about your impending arrival. He has already sent out spies to gather intelligence on the activities of the English and Arcot troops in the region. He will be able to advise you on the best approach to drive our enemies out. Your expertise in the knowledge of the terrain and the populace of the region would be extremely useful here.'

'Syed Karki's tactical expertise is greatly appreciated. We will utilize all our experience and knowledge of our motherland to vanquish our enemies,' Velu Nachiyar promised.

'I would also advise you to get in touch with your allies in the Marava country and rally them for a final push against the English. Their loyalties would make our passage much easier,' Purnaiah continued.

'I will have my diplomats alert all the palegars, nayakas and other chieftains about the final push. We have good relations with them. With the addition of the Mysuru troops to our ranks, we are bound to have the local chieftains rally on our side. Our numbers are bound to swell with additions from them.'

'Good. Now that it's settled, I would like to shift over to something more personal, your highness, with your permission, of course. I came to know to that you arrived here in Srirangapatna accompanied only by your two diplomats. Your journey to Srirangapatna must have been extremely risky. Traversing through hostile territory without any protection is akin to playing with death. I am amazed at your courage and tenacity.'

'I am a victim of my circumstances, General Purnaiah. I have fallen on bad times, and it was under these conditions that I chose to undertake this perilous journey. But in the end, it was fruitful and, with Mysuru's help, I should be able to make all these efforts and sacrifices worthwhile.'

'Are you planning to go to Dindigul alone, your highness? Purnaiah asked, concerned.

'I am afraid so.'

'Well, if I may, I would consider it an honour if you would accept an armed escort, which I will provide you at my personal expense.'

'That's extremely gracious of you. It would be my privilege to accept your armed escort.'

'Very well, then, I shall make all the preparations for your departure, your highness. I hope to see you next time on the throne of Sivaganga.'

Post-monsoon of 1778, Fort St George, Madras

Sir Thomas Rumbold, the governor of the Madras Presidency, was sitting in his office behind a large brown teak table, going through his daily letters. His two writers were on the opposite side of the office, right next to the door. A young English officer sat on the opposite side of the teak table, listening to the governor.

Picking up a letter, Rumbold began, 'I have received an update from our spies in Srirangapatna. The guerrilla leader of Sivaganga has gone to Nawab Hyder Ali seeking help to reclaim the kingdom.'

'We have ammunition stored in the Sivaganga fort under the guard of a small garrison. Would you like to strengthen the garrison in the fort, sir?' the young English officer asked.

'There has been a guerrilla problem festering in that region for many years now,' Rumbold replied. 'We are not even getting much revenue from there. I don't want to invest any more money. Major General Smith and Lieutenant Colonel Bonjour captured Sivaganga but could not subdue the insurgency that came after we took over the kingdom. Both are now happily retired, back home in England, with Bonjour even lining his pockets with Arcot gold before leaving, while I am left here to deal with their mess.'

'What do you propose we do, sir?'

'Nothing. We don't even know if Nawab Hyder Ali has offered those people help. If the nawab were to make a move, he would probably attack Arcot directly. Now, that would be a problem. The Arcot nawab provides us with a lot of men, money and other resources. We need to protect Arcot. So, I would rather focus on Arcot than waste my resources on a frontier province. I will not augment our troops in Sivaganga. I don't think we will face an attack there.'

'Yes, sir.'

Rubbing his chin, Rumbold continued, 'Actually, we can benefit from this event. We can forward our own interests using the recent actions of this rebel leader from Sivaganga.'

He instructed his writers, 'Draft a letter to the prince of Arcot, informing him about the rebel leader's visit to Srirangapatna. Ask him for an additional amount of money to secure the southern borders of Arcot against Mysuru's supposed machinations.'

'And I presume we would not be doing anything at the southern borders of Arcot, sir?' the young English officer asked.

'Of course not.'

Post-monsoon of 1778, the crown prince's palace in Arcot

Ameer-ul-Umara was grooming his well-trimmed beard in front of a large, ornate French mirror in his personal quarters, as a courtier read out the letter from Sir Thomas Rumbold.

'The only constant with the English is the never-ending ask for money,' the prince said through gritted teeth.

He moved away from the mirror to sit in a chair. Still looking at his reflection, the prince sank deeper into his thoughts.

Just a few weeks back, the English said Sivaganga was fully under their control, and now they say everything could be lost to Mysuru. The English have told me that they have a good presence there. A good number of my soldiers are there as well. Why would Mysuru attack Sivaganga? How strange of Mysuru to aid a helpless woman for a piece of worthless land? After all these years, Velu Nachiyar is yet to be captured, and now she suddenly surfaces in Mysuru! How did she even get to Mysuru? How did she traverse through the country without getting caught? What were the English troops doing? What were my soldiers doing? People seem to have long forgotten the bounty on the former queen's head.

The prince of Arcot got back to grooming his beard, while the courtier stood silently with the letter in his hand.

I have extracted all the money I could from that wretched place. I have secured my position as the crown prince here in Arcot. My father has given me control of all lands south of Trichy. My goals are met. But I still need the military aid of the English for the future. It's better to be in their good books and humour them.

Satisfied with his beard and his flailing thoughts, Ameer-ul-Umara responded to the courtier, 'Well, there must be some grain of truth in what the English are saying. Draft a letter to the governor acquiescing to his request. Also, send a message to my treasurer to arrange for the transfer the money to Madras.'

'Yes, my lord.'

The courtier bowed to his master and exited the room. Ameer-ul-Umara got up from his chair and went back to the mirror to inspect his final look.

10

The winter of 1778, Dindigul

THE BIG HILL IN DINDIGUL LOOKED LIKE A PILLOW MADE OF stone, and the fort on top of it looked even more delicate. But as Rani Velu Nachiyar, her two diplomats and the armed escort got closer, the true imposing nature of the fort dawned on them. Civilians resided in the bustling town at the foot of the hill. The soldier's barracks and an entire military infrastructure were loomed over them. The town of Dindigul itself was surrounded by tall hills all around, with only three points for ingress and egress.

The queen grew surprised upon observing the terrain.

I always wondered how Mysuru could control a place so far from Srirangapatna with such ease. Now, having seen the terrain in person, it is clear to me how extremely difficult it is to dislodge the Mysuru troops from here. To top it off, the sheer strength of the Mysuru army is sufficient to dictate terms to the neighbouring kingdoms of Dindigul. No wonder the English ravaged all lands south of the Kaveri but stayed away from Dindigul province. Even the Arcot soldiers wouldn't dare enter this region. All the palegars and nayakas in the region, including our very own Gopal

Nayakar, swear loyalty to the commander of Dindigul, making it all the more difficult for anyone to challenge the kingdom. With the help of the Dindigul commander, we will surely turn the tables on the English.

The horses that this travelling party had mounted trudged slowly on the granite rocks as they followed the winding path to the entrance of the fort. The gates were already open; Velu Nachiyar was expected. The soldier guarding the gate guided the party to the fort commandant's, *khilladar*'s, office.

Syed Karki was dictating something to his writer when the rani entered his office. The commander of the Dindigul army was a doe-eyed, thin, young man. He sported a clean-shaven look with a thick, neatly combed crop of hair. He looked regal in his bright white silk kurta that was held by a green cummerbund at the waist. Just like the nawab of Mysuru, he also did not wear any jewellery. On seeing the queen, a bright smile lit up his face.

'Welcome, your highness,' he exclaimed. 'I have been expecting you. Please have a seat.'

Thanking the commander, Velu Nachiyar handed over the letters of credence from Purnaiah to him. Accepting them respectfully, he passed them on to his writer for record-keeping.

'I presume you must be tired from the journey. I suggest you rest for a while before we discuss the nitty-gritties of our upcoming operation.'

'The journey has merely been holding me back from starting our fight against the English, Commander Syed,' the queen said with a smile.

An impressed Syed Karki replied, 'I share your enthusiasm, your highness. We can start right now, or we could wait for your generals to join us before we chalk out a plan of action.'

Looking at her diplomats, Velu Nachiyar said, 'My diplomats will leave immediately to get them here. I expect my generals to arrive here in a few weeks. But I would like to know our next steps right away. I can hardly wait to quench my thirst for justice.'

'Very well. The plan is quite simple, your highness. Our primary objective is to capture Sivaganga. In order to achieve this goal, we need to clear the field between Dindigul and Sivaganga of enemy forces. In fact, we must get rid of all hostile forces on the field before we get moving.'

'Do you have any intelligence on the resistance we could face?'

'Our enemies are mostly concentrated in one or two camps. If we manage to clear these camps and drive them away, I think we will have an unobstructed path to Sivaganga. Of course, all of this is subject to the local palegars and nayakas remaining loyal to you and allowing us to move unhindered.'

'I will ensure we have unhindered access during our march, Commander Syed. I will despatch a few of my diplomats to the palegars and nayakas of the region at the outset.'

'Yes, I would recommend that we have them on our side before we proceed.'

Rani Velu Nachiyar's excitement tempered a bit. Quite a few things had to be taken care of before launching the final assault and it would all take time. But she agreed to Syed Karki's proposal with a silent nod.

Syed Karki continued, 'Well, until we have the pledges from the palegars, and before your generals are here, we can take care of other things. Firstly, would you like to inspect the troops that are stationed here, your highness?'

'Yes, absolutely!'

Velu Nachiyar stepped out of the office with the commander. The entire fort was essentially a military camp with just a handful of civilians.

Looking around the fort, quite a few things surprised the queen.

'Are they French?' she asked, looking at a group of white-skinned people nearby.

'They are, your highness. Our French engineers are responsible for the upkeep of the fort. If you look over there, you'll find French grenadiers, who form the spear head of our forces. They are quite adept at storming fortifications and are hoping to see some action in the coming months. We also have some French officers who lead various units of our troops. Mysuru has a strong relationship with France, and there is no love lost between the English and the French. They are thirsting for the blood of the English just as much as us, your highness.'

The rani walked over to the engineers and began conversing with them in fluent French. The engineers were pleasantly surprised at the linguistic skills of the queen and answered her questions with enthusiasm. She enquired about their ranks and the general situation in Puducherry. She then promised them a chance at revenge against their mortal enemies. The French engineers saluted the queen with zeal, looking forward to battling it out with the English.

A surprised Syed Karki began, 'I had heard that our nawab was impressed with your Kannada-speaking skills. Now, I see the same prowess albeit in a different language. I must say, I am amazed by your linguistic capabilities, your highness.'

The queen of Sivaganga accepted the compliment with a gracious nod.

Velu Nachiyar was guided through the barracks. There were numerous soldiers in the small field in front of the barracks, participating in a drill. Every soldier was in a similar uniform and they all had a musket in their hands. Every movement of the soldiers was in perfect coordination.

Impressed by the discipline being displayed by the soldiers in the drill, the queen asked Syed Karki, 'Will they be fighting for us?'

'Yes, your highness. A total of 5,000 men each from our infantry and cavalry will be fighting side by side with you. Let's visit the stables and inspect our famed Kuzzaks. They are the best light cavalry of the land.'

Moving ahead to the stables, it was quite a sight to see so many horses. The rani found it difficult to fathom the fact that so many horses were housed and fed on top of a hill.

'How do you feed these horses?'

'We have enough grass around the fort, your highness. Sometimes we take them downhill for grazing as well. Your question brings up an important point. I am already in the process of procuring supplies for our operation. We wouldn't want long supply lines that could be attacked during our expedition. So, I am stocking up for the entirety of the operation. We need to be rigorous with respect to supplies. I don't want to leave anything to chance.'

Rani Velu Nachiyar looked at the Dindigul commander, impressed.

This boy means business. I have a pair of steady hands with me for this campaign.

With the tour complete, Syed Karki escorted Velu Nachiyar to the guest quarters.

'I have received money from the Srirangapatna treasury,' he said. 'You already know that Mysuru will be issuing 400 pagodas every month for the upkeep of your army. I will bear the expenses of my army on my own. With this, we will have everything to take on the English and Arcot. We will soon get back Sivaganga to you, your highness,' he said with a slight bow.

'Thank you, Commander Syed,' the queen said sincerely.

Within the next few weeks, the Maruthu brothers arrived in Dindigul. The Sivaganga army and its generals also moved to the base of the hill fort. Vellachi was also brought along to the safe environs of Dindigul where she would now have access to better doctors and medications and, more importantly, her mother. Messengers sent out by Velu Nachiyar to the palegars and nayakas were returning with good news. Most of them pledged loyalty to the queen. Fence-sitters were now firmly on the side of Sivaganga, what with the strength of the Mysuru army now secured. Some of them even sent their own men to augment the forces of Sivaganga. Everything was finally coming together now.

After the arrival of the Sivaganga army at the Dindigul fort, Syed Karki, Velu Nachiyar and the Maruthu brothers spent the next few months finalizing the logistics, procuring and distributing supplies amongst the soldiers, paying the merchants and deploying scouts among other things to get themselves ready for the upcoming expedition. Once all these activities were completed, the group convened in the khilladar's office to confirm the war plan before heading out of the fort.

Syed Karki was providing finer details.

'A majority of the Arcot's forces are presently camped outside Madurai. There are a sizeable number of English soldiers at Kalayar Koil. A smaller contingent is stationed at Sivaganga as well. There are pockets of sentries across the land, which isn't a cause for concern at present. We can sweep them away during our movement. We need to clear out the forces at Madurai and Kalayar Koil before making any move on Sivaganga. Unless we clear them, we run the risk of being crammed between enemy forces.'

Chinna Maruthu Pandiyar concurred with Syed Karki. 'We shall split into two groups and attack our enemies at Madurai and Kalayar Koil simultaneously. We can then rendezvous at a chosen location and attack the English at Sivaganga.'

Velu Nachiyar disagreed, 'We have a higher chance of success if we hit each of these places with the full strength of our forces. Our enemies' forces are quite formidable; let's not take them lightly. If we split up, we risk greater fatalities in both places. We can eliminate our enemies at Madurai and Kalayar Koil one after another. There is a fair amount of distance between the two places, as they lie on either side of Sivaganga. Our groups will not be able to come to the rescue of the other, if needed, on the battlefield. I would prefer we take them out one at a time.'

Syed Karki weighed the rani's arguments and soon felt convinced. Chinna Maruthu Pandiyar too considered the queen's argument and agreed to the plan. It would take them longer to reach Sivaganga this way, but they would certainly diminish their losses.

The commander continued with his intelligence report.

'The Arcot camp outside Madurai isn't equipped with many

defence fortifications. We wouldn't need any siege equipment. The terrain is flat as well. So, our cavalry will have an edge over the Arcot infantry.'

The younger Maruthu general was impressed with Syed Karki's battle tactics and his general know-how. He looked at the queen, who merely smiled in agreement.

Periya Maruthu Pandiyar, who was listening impatiently all this while, suddenly cut in, 'All this planning and plotting is fine. When do we actually fight? I am baying for English blood!'

Syed Karki looked at the queen and said, 'When her highness gives the order, we move.'

A charged-up Rani Velu Nachiyar declared, 'We are ready to go!'

Between loud cheers, she continued, 'We will first attack our enemies who are based near Madurai. They are the closest to us – a few days' march from here. More importantly, they are the weaker of the two factions. They will be easy pickings for us and a good start to our campaign to take back Sivaganga.'

Periya Maruthu Pandiyar couldn't stop grinning.

'So, it's the Arcot soldiers who will first face our wrath,' he proclaimed. 'Let's move out of the fort at an auspicious time and take the first step in winning back our homeland.'

Before the monsoon of 1779, outside Madurai

Dressed in traditional Mughal infantry attire – blue tops and greens pants – with English muskets in their hands and gunpowder tumbrils tied to their hips, the Arcot infantry looked nervous as they lined up close to each other, while a small cavalry unit protected the flanks. Their general was right behind them, with his small, personal cavalry guarding him. His face looked grim. His infantry line wasn't deep enough to engage the enemy in a sustained battle.

The swift movement of the combined Mysuru–Sivaganga armies towards Madurai had forced the Arcot army camped in the region to offer battle. The speed of the combined army seemed to have caught them so off guard and so far a way from Madurai that they decided to go into battle at the first point of contact with no thought for a tactical retreat to safer grounds.

A little ahead, the larger Mysuru and Sivaganga armies were standing in tight formation. Their flanks too were covered by their cavalry, and their numbers were significantly more than what their enemies had expected, so much so, that the Arcot general could not even estimate the depth of their lines. The Arcot soldiers were evidently outnumbered by their opponents.

On top of the numerical disadvantage was the dry, flat terrain, with a scattering of dried brown grass that offered no protection. It was a level playing field where everyone could see each other in the absence of any hills or trees. The Arcot soldiers were well aware of their unfavourable situation; they were on their own. But there was something more, beyond these disadvantages, that brought fear into their hearts. It was their history with the Mysuru army. Arcot had always faced decimation in every battle against Mysuru. And things were not looking much different here.

Meanwhile, on the other side of the battlefield, Commander Syed Karki was calm and steady as he spoke with his officers, offering jokes and light banter. Even the soldiers in the infantry were unruffled. It seemed like any other day, one which they knew the outcome of beforehand. The Dindigul commander, along with Rani Velu Nachiyar and the Maruthu brothers, was stationed behind the army line, guarded by his personal cavalry and the all-women Udaiyal army led by Kuyili. The Sivaganga leaders and soldiers were a bit tense in comparison, but there was unshakeable confidence in their eyes. It was the first big battle they were facing after many years; it could make or break them.

The Mysuru soldiers occupied the front lines of the army. The Sivaganga soldiers were on the flanks, between the Mysuru infantry and cavalry. Another large contingent stood behind the Mysuru infantry, comprising the local men drawn from the folds of loyal palegars – some hired mercenaries and zealous villagers who wanted to fight under the banner of the queen. This ragtag bunch was in the thousands and formed the bulk of this army, but the true fighting forces – soldiers from Mysuru and Sivaganga – were in the front. The Mysuru soldiers were well armoured and armed with muskets. Next to them, the Sivaganga soldiers were lightly armoured and equipped with valaris and aruvals, while the group at the very back wielded an assortment of weapons, ranging from aruvals to ordinary farm tools.

The Sivaganga group was brimming with excitement with many troopers shouting at the top of their lungs, cursing their opponents and waving their aruvals, a stark contrast from the Mysuru infantry.

The foot soldiers of Mysuru were protected by the Kuzzaks. The cavalry was evenly divided into two units to protect the two flanks. They were completely focused on their enemies ahead, ignoring the aggressive shouts from the Sivaganga soldiers and holding their horses steady.

With the Arcot and Mysuru–Sivaganga armies standing opposite each other, it was time to make the first move. Syed Karki instructed the officer in charge to get the infantry ready. 'Load your muskets! Get in position!' the officer ordered.

On cue, the soldiers filled their barrels with gun powder and slotted the shots. With the muskets loaded, lines of troopers resumed their battle-ready positions.

Looking at the rani, the commander said, 'Our enemies are not well trained with muskets. We will wait for them to move forward and get in range before initiating the attack.'

'What if they don't move forward?' Chinna Maruthu Pandiyar asked.

'They will,' Syed Karki said with a smile.

The confidence in his reply was sufficient to convince Velu Nachiyar. She looked ahead at the Arcot army, waiting for them to make the first move.

Seeing the Mysuru infantry load their muskets, the Arcot general ordered his soldiers to do the same. Despite being more technologically advanced, the Arcot infantry took a lot more time to get in position than their Mysuru counterparts. They were clearly not trained well enough to handle their weaponry. Where the Mysuru infantrymen displayed patience, the Sivaganga soldiers were starting to get impatient, standing next to the Mysuru infantry with their valaris and waiting for their opponents to attack. They were not used to this level of discipline and order and were rather well acquainted with a simpler approach: when one sees the enemy, one attacks.

Standing still on the battlefield was not part of their warfare. Some raced forward without permission and threw their valaris in impatience, taking aim at the enemy cavalry on the left flank. Even though most of the valaris fell short, a few that hit their targets slashed the horses, agitating the horsemen.

An angry Periya Maruthu Pandiyar shouted at his men, 'Halt! Don't attack until you are ordered to do so!'

He charged his horse through the lines of the Sivaganga army to keep them in check. The soldiers were steadied, but their actions had an unintended impact.

Despite suffering minimal damage, the Arcot cavalry on the left flank became unsettled and grew angered by the attack. They wanted to charge at their aggressors. The Arcot general too thought that the valari attack was the opening salvo of the battle and ordered his infantry to move forward to get in range. Without waiting to steady the left flank and with no one to hold them back, the opponents charged.

The sudden change in action didn't seem to deter the Dindigul commander. As the cavalry moved in range, he signalled his officer. The officer barked the order, 'Fire!'

Within seconds, a hail of shots hit the Arcot cavalry, scattering them all over the field. As the Mysuru infantry's front line stepped back to reload their muskets, its second line came forward to fire the next round of shots. A sizeable number of the Arcot cavalry collapsed. The remaining horsemen lost courage and began retreating in disarray. With the third round of fire, there was hardly anyone left standing in between the two armies.

Seeing the opening in the Arcot army, Commander Syed shouted, 'Their flank is exposed! Order our right flank in!'

The Mysuru cavalry's right flank darted in a long-winding

path to avoid the enemy's musket fire. The Arcot infantry could not help but break their formation to brace themselves against the onslaught. Periya Maruthu Pandiyar now ordered the Sivaganga soldiers to charge. They quickly did and unleashed their weapons on the enemy infantry. Sharp valaris rained down on the Arcot soldiers, slicing through their heads, necks, hands and legs. Defenceless against this unexpected attack, the maimed soldiers were unable to move back into formation. Just as the last valari came down, the full fury of the Mysuru cavalry charged towards them. The impact was brutal. Many soldiers were trampled under the hooves of the Mysuru horses. Chaos ran deep through the Arcot ranks.

The Arcot general was not a brave man. Seeing the fatalities in his infantry, he retreated in haste. His move took out the last ounce of morale left in his army. The cavalry on the right flank was too disengaged from its position to retreat. Upon seeing the other flank disengage, Syed Karki ordered his left flank, 'The Arcot cavalry is retreating! Chase them! Slaughter them all!'

They took off, chasing the retreating Arcot cavalry. The Arcot infantry found themselves all alone amid attacks from the Mysuru cavalry on one side and the Sivaganga soldiers on the other.

Syed Karki looked at Periya Maruthu Pandiyar and said with a smirk, 'They are all yours.'

The big man grinned and ordered the rest of the Sivaganga soldiers to charge.

The Arcot line was now in utter disarray. They ran back helter-skelter. The Sivaganga soldiers, armed only with their aruvals, were able to easily outpace their enemies and began slashing them with impunity. The Arcot soldiers were falling like cut grass. Periya Maruthu Pandiyar too joined the battle now as he scythed the hapless men. It was not a battle anymore, rather a full-blown slaughter.

In midst of all this chaos, Commander Syed had not lost sight of his goal. He ordered his cavalry's right flank, currently engaged with the Arcot infantry, to instead chase the retreating enemy cavalry.

'Don't let any of them escape alive!'

The cavalry disengaged and turned their attention to the retreating cavalry and its general. They charged in their direction in earnest. With the cavalries chasing each other, soon it was just men on the ground that were left fighting.

Syed Karki was still stationed behind with his guards, along with the leaders of the Sivaganga army, except for the older Maruthu general, who was evidently enjoying the fight. Rani Velu Nachiyar asked, 'That was quick. I was expecting a tougher fight. Would they be regrouping again by any chance to face us again?'

'Regroup? Their infantry has been decimated. Mysuru has the fastest cavalry in the land. Our enemies will be dead by the end of the day. I will be surprised if the Arcot general makes it out alive. It's not a battle anymore, your highness, it is a hunt and the Mysuru Kuzzaks love hunting,' Syed Karki said with a smirk.

By dusk, the commander had moved his troops to a safer grounds and had set up camp. The light cavalry had also returned with expected news – the battalion of the Arcot cavalry had been eliminated.

The Sivaganga soldiers had tasted victory after a very long time. It was cause for celebration. Spirits in the camp were high as everyone sang and danced. The Maruthu brothers too joined the revelries.

Velu Nachiyar was alone with Syed Karki in the dining area, having a supper of warm gruel.

The commander said joyfully, 'This was easier than I expected, your highness. I would recommend we proceed at the earliest to eliminate the other army at Kalayar Koil.'

'The first step was the easiest, Commander Syed. It will progressively get more difficult from here on. We need to have a robust plan before we take on the English at Kalayar Koil.'

11

The winter of 1779, Sivaganga

SYED KARKI WAS IN THE MAIN TENT WITH VELU NACHIYAR AND the Maruthu brothers. Kuyili stood guard outside with the women bodyguards. The Dindigul commander was putting together the plan for the next attack.

'The English are a different breed,' he was saying. 'They are better trained, have superior battle tactics, the best weapons, and don't back down despite overwhelming odds.'

He paused for the audience to absorb the information. There was trepidation on everybody's faces. But that didn't faze him. In his usual calm demeanour, he continued, 'They would have already heard about our attack near Madurai. If we give them enough time, they might come after us. We need to maintain the element of surprise, but it will be more challenging after the first battle.'

Chinna Maruthu Pandiyar interrupted Syed Karki, 'Why is that? They wouldn't know when and where we would attack them.'

The queen was quick with her answer.

'The English are now sure of an impending attack, and they have more resilient officers in their fold. They would have definitely prepared contingency plans to mitigate the impact of our attack. We cannot rely on surprise alone. We need something more.'

Periya Maruthu Pandiyar asked, 'So, what do you propose?'

'This will be a simple and straightforward fight,' Velu Nachiyar began. 'We would be pitting our men, arms and battle tactics against theirs. Syed Karki's intelligence is a few days' old, but he tells me that the English are still camped at Kalayar Koil. This could mean two things – either they have decided to stay put and defend Kalayar Koil, or they are getting ready to march against us.' She stopped and looked at the commander to fill them in.

'I know from experience that the English are slow in moving camps,' the commander spoke. 'So, we might have to wait a few days to understand their intentions. But I propose we attack them at Kalayar Koil rather than somewhere in the middle. With this approach, we can drive away the last major enemy force outside the Sivaganga fort and take back Kalayar Koil as well. Or we move to secure grounds and wait for the English to attack us first.'

The room remained silent. A call had to be made.

Syed Karki and the Maruthu brothers looked towards the rani expectantly. She was in a pensive state.

Kalayar Koil is the place where I lost my beloved husband and kingdom. This is the place which sent me on my exile in the bowels of perdition. Justice will be mine only if I pry it back from the bloodied hands of the English. Kalayar Koil must become a battlefield again. Only then will my husband and Sivaganga's honour be restored.'

'We will attack the English at Kalayar Koil,' Rani Velu Nachiyar said resolutely. Looking at the commander, she continued, 'Please make preparations to march to the town.'

Happy with the queen's decision, Syed Karki announced, 'Yes, your highness. We will break camp tomorrow and begin our march. But there are a few things we need to address before confronting the English.'

'What are those?' the Maruthu brothers asked in unison.

'Kalayar Koil lies beyond Sivaganga. For us to start marching from here, we would need to take a more circuitous route to the town, avoiding the Sivaganga fort on our way. The English will be swarming all around it. It would be good if we could ensure a safe passage up to Kalayar Koil. If you could get your loyal palegars and nayakas along that route onboard too, we can remain at full strength when we face the English.'

The queen ordered the Maruthu brothers, 'Peri Pandi, Chinna Pandi, you both must go ahead and work with the palegars and nayakas to ascertain a safe passage for the troops, just like you did before our battle with the Arcot troops. We will follow right behind you.'

Chinna Maruthu Pandiyar replied, 'Yes, my queen. We will start right away and clear a path south of Sivaganga. It should be the quickest way to Kalayar Koil.'

Periya Maruthu Pandiyar was already up. The generals took their leave and stepped out of the camp. The older Maruthu brother signalled the stable boys to get their horses.

The next morning, the queen and the commander were awakened by Kuyili and some villagers. The ever-smiling Kuyili began, 'Amma, Peri Pandi anna has sent these villagers. They will guide us to the next village. The villagers have also told me that we will have reinforcements along our path.'

Syed Karki was quite impressed.

'We have a safe path and reinforcements. I say, things are off to an excellent start!'

Guided by the villagers, the entourage soon reached the next village to the south of Kalayar Koil. Here they were greeted by auxiliary troops offered by the local palegar. The Maruthu brothers were nowhere to be found. They had gone further ahead to ensure a safe passage for the queen, her entourage and the troops.

Despite being on a longer and more roundabout route, the troops kept moving with no difficulties. Their strength was being augmented by new auxiliary troops joining them every passing day, which was a testament to the conviction of the local chieftains in the queen and the upcoming battle with the English. The Maruthu brothers rendezvoused with the augmented troops at the final camp before entering Kalayar Koil.

The night was cool, and a pleasant breeze was blowing through the camp. Velu Nachiyar couldn't sleep. Her nervousness about the next day made her restless. Finally giving up, she got up and came out of her tent. The winter sky was clear, and the stars were shimmering. The night was serene and seemed to soothe the queen's nerves. She saw the torch outside Syed Karki's tent still burning. *He is still awake*, she thought and walked up to his tent. On seeing the queen approach, the guard posted outside the tent went inside to inform the commander. Within a few moments, he ushered the queen inside.

The commander was finishing up some letters. He kept them aside when the queen entered the tent. He pre-empted the queen's first question, 'I am writing a letter to the nawab of Mysuru. I am apprising him of the situation here, your highness.'

'How do you perceive our present situation?'

'Well-balanced, your highness,' he said plainly.

Already nervous about the day ahead, this lukewarm response from the Dindigul commander did little to calm the queen's nerves.

'Why do you say so, Syed?' she asked, sounding a little distraught. 'You seem to lack your earlier confidence. Do you think it will be hard for us to overcome our enemies tomorrow?'

Syed Karki immediately realized that he had frayed her nerves at a critical juncture.

'There is nothing to worry about, your highness,' he began. 'We have a strong army to take on the English. But we cannot predict or control the actions of our enemy, and we cannot predict our fate.'

'Nobody knows the outcome until the battle is over. But we all seek glory and none of us wants to die. I think that should be enough motivation for us to do our best. But you seem demotivated, and that concerns me,' the queen stated matter-of-factly.

The commander's objective approach did little to calm down the queen. Trying hard to retain her optimism, she continued, 'We have strengthened our armies with sizeable reinforcements. I am sure we stand a better chance of winning tomorrow with this recent addition. What do you say?'

Syed Karki's objectivity was still intact. In a flat tone, he replied, 'These auxiliary troops don't stand a chance against a determined and better-equipped enemy like that of the

English. But it is always good to have a larger number on our side.'

His poor opinion of the new auxiliary troops angered Velu Nachiyar. She raised her voice, 'These men are willing to lay down their lives for me, Commander Syed. I am sure they will stand their ground against those English sepoys.'

Sensing the conversation going awry, Syed Karki attempted a course correction.

'Of course, your highness. I never doubted that. They will be extremely valuable in our battle tomorrow.'

The rani was not convinced.

'You do not seem confident. Are the English so formidable that we won't be able to drive them out of our lands?'

'On the contrary, it is the English that need to be afraid of us, your highness. We have the best and the bravest soldiers on our side. Rest assured; we will have them at the end of our bayonets before the day is finished,' Commander Syed pronounced vehemently.

A small smile broke on Rani Velu Nachiyar's face. The renewed confidence that the queen was able to stir in the Dindigul commander was sufficient to ease her nerves. Syed Karki also felt encouraged and was relieved to see the queen relax.

'It is the way I have been trained, your highness,' he continued after a pause. 'The nawab of Mysuru always asks for an objective assessment of every situation, no matter our assurance of a positive outcome. So, the other generals and I have been trained to offer details devoid of all emotion. I realize that it is not the right way to communicate on all occasions. But I assure you, our strength and numbers will surely stir fear within the English. With the augmentation of the troops, thanks to your loyalists, we will have a definite upper hand in the battle.' Velu Nachiyar could sense the conviction in his voice.

'Thank you, Syed,' she calmly said.

'I would request you to sleep well, your highness. We will capture Sivaganga much before the next winter and see you back on the throne of your kingdom.'

Velu Nachiyar bid goodbye to the commander and went back to her tent. With her mind much calmer now, she was able to drift off to sleep soon.

As dawn arrived, the troops broke camp and ate a good breakfast. Scouts returned with news that the English were making their stand on the edge of Kalayar Koil, just outside the thick forests that bordered the town. Syed Karki split the army into multiple columns and ordered them to march towards Kalayar Koil.

With the army beginning their march, he called for a final meeting with the queen and the Maruthu brothers to plan their course of action.

'The English have taken up a strategic position just north of Kalayar Koil. They have the advantage of an elevated ground and the protection of the forest behind them. Another battalion of the Arcot cavalry has been deployed to defend their flanks. We may need to change our tactics slightly. We need to find a way to outflank them or dislodge them from their position.'

Chinna Maruthu Pandiyar offered a suggestion, 'Why don't we get behind them? That would be much better than outflanking them. By attacking their rear, we can dislodge them from their position for sure.'

'But what about the thick forest. How do you propose we overcome this natural barrier?'

A smug smile spread over the general's face.

'We know this place like the back of our hands, Commander Syed Karki. Our troops were born and brought up in this region. We will be able to get behind their backs with ease.'

The commander was sold on this suggestion. He asked for more details, 'If we divert the Sivaganga troops, how long will it take for you to get behind them?'

'The path is long and we will be a little slow in the forest. We will need a couple more hours.'

'Then the other troops will have to slow down their approach to the hill to buy you more time. We might also have to absorb some blows from the English until you reach your position. We should be able to handle that. Alright, with that decided, let's split up and trap the English between our troops.'

The Maruthu brothers disengaged the lightly armoured Sivaganga troops from the main column and had them move towards the forest. Rani Velu stayed on with Syed Karki and his army and gradually moved ahead towards Kalayar Koil.

The town looked desolate as the Mysuru troops entered it. With the English not wanting any of the civilians rallying round the incoming troops, they had been cleared out. The Mysuru troops snaked their way from the southern edge of the town to its northern end. The English troops were standing on a gradient with their backs to the forest. Wearing their customary red coats and white bottoms, they stood out against the dull green forest of Kalayar Koil. The Mysuru soldiers, meanwhile, in their all-cream uniform looked unimpressive compared to their enemies. As the last of the Mysuru troops made their way to the sloped arena, they were still out of range of the English muskets.

Syed Karki ordered his officers, 'Quickly get everyone in formation!'

The troops formed multiple lines, with the cavalry positioned at the ends.

Even though the battalion of Arcot cavalry protecting the rear of English troops was small and didn't pose a major challenge, Syed Karki knew that his own horses would give him a minimal advantage on this uneven field. With trees jutting out all around, the horses had very little space for a charge or for manoeuvring. This was essentially a battle of the infantries.

While Syed Karki's troops were slightly fatigued by the uphill march, the English were well rested and primed to go. The English officer, not waiting for his opponents to settle down, ordered his troops to begin moving downhill until they were in range. By then, the first few lines of the Mysuru infantry were also ready with their muskets loaded and pointed in the direction of the English. As soon as the English sepoys were within range, Syed Karki ordered his men, 'Fire!'

Within the next few seconds, multiple shots flew past the English, with many a sepoy collapsing. The English captain ordered the front line of his infantry to get into position and fire.

Sounds of multiple shots rented the air. The battlefield smelled of gunpowder, with a thick black blanket of smoke covering the grounds. Line after line of soldiers, on either side, fired shots in succession. Soldiers crumbled on both sides. But none yielded; the firing went on for hours.

The English ran out of gunpowder first. The sepoys were ordered, 'Fix your bayonets!'

Syed Karki saw the sepoys fixing their bayonets and quickly ordered his men, except those in the first two lines, to fix their as well. As the first two Mysuru lines continued firing, the English sepoys in the front took the brunt of the musket shots. Once their muskets were ready, the English officer shouted his order, 'Charge!'

The English infantry ran down the uneven ground with bayonets pointed towards the Mysuru troops. The Mysuru infantry continued firing, holding their positions. Despite taking multiple hits, the sepoys didn't slow down. They gathered momentum as they came down. Syed Karki quickly ordered his front lines to withdraw.

'Charge!' Syed Karki ordered the successive lines.

The Mysuru infantry now ran uphill to meet their enemies. The clashing of metal, under the haze of gunpowder smoke, competed with the shouts of the soldiers. A scrimmage ensued between the two contingents; neither yielded. Despite their marginal numerical superiority, the Mysuru soldiers, fighting in such close quarters with the English sepoys, were left with almost no advantage. The cavalry was no help on either side.

At the height of the battle, Syed Karki noticed the Arcot cavalry suddenly turn back and go inside the forest. The keen commander instructed an officer, 'Something is afoot. Their cavalry has gone inside. Get ours ready.'

As the Mysuru cavalry was getting ready, a raft of shining metal valaris shot out of the forest into the sky, dazzling in the bright sun and then raining right down on the English soldiers. Their sharp blades cut through the back line of the English sepoys. Some of the valaris lodged themselves in their necks, some others on their hands and legs and many slashed their backs.

An excited rani exclaimed, 'They are here! Our mighty generals have finally come to our rescue!'

The Sivaganga men came thundering down the forest with aruvals in their hands, which they lunged straight at the sepoys at the rear of the English contingent. The Arcot cavalrymen furiously slashed their swords, chopping away several Sivaganga soldiers, hoping to block their charge against the English. But they were easily outnumbered and managed to bog down a mere number of the charging troops. Worse was to follow, for the Mysuru cavalry was now ready.

Commander Syed ordered his cavalry, 'Engage those Arcot horses!'

The Mysuru horses negotiated the tight space, bypassing the battle that was underway, to reach the forest where Arcot horses were attacking the Sivaganga men. As the Mysuru cavalry moved up, an officer came upon an Englishman lying in a pool of his own blood with a valari stuck deep in his head. He immediately recognized the man. Chopping its head off, he carried it back to Syed Karki.

'My Lord! The English captain has been killed! They are without their leader now!' he said, offering the severed head as proof.

The arrival of the Sivaganga soldiers boosted the morale of

the Mysuru troops. The English sepoys were now crammed between the aruval-wielding men and the Mysuru soldiers. They were unaware of the death of their leader and, despite the odds slowly turning against them, continued fighting with zeal.

With this new information from his officer, Syed Karki knew that he now had the decisive advantage. He wanted to finish the battle. Turning to Velu Nachiyar, he said, 'We need to break the morale of the English, your highness. We need to show them that we have killed their leader. This is bound to break their determination.'

The rani nodded in agreement. Throwing the head of the English officer towards Periya Maruthu Pandiyar, Syed Karki declared, 'Let's get back into battle and send this message.'

'Yes,' Periya Maruthu Pandiyar bellowed.

Syed Karki and Periya Maruthu Pandiyar went into battle with their personal guards. They began cutting through the English ranks. Syed Karki's officers began shouting, 'The English leader has been killed! The English leader has been killed! Finish them off!'

Just as Syed Karki had anticipated, the morale of the English sepoys took a hit. They started yielding to the pressure from the Mysuru infantry. To make matters worse, Periya Maruthu Pandiyar lobbed the head of the officer into the middle of the field. The English lost their fighting spirit in the blink of an eye. Breaking away from the fight, they retreated into the town and beyond. The Mysuru cavalry began chasing them, but their commander had other intentions.

'Halt! Nobody chases them! We will get them again.'

Periya Maruthu Pandiyar came over to him. 'Let's finish them. Why are we holding back? Let's get them before they escape!'

'We have taken losses, too. We cannot afford any more. The English are a spent force now. They will not cause more trouble. Let them run.'

The Maruthu general was disappointed and angry.

'We can't let them escape alive. They need to be slaughtered for what they have done so far. Let's pursue them,' he urged.

Periya Maruthu Pandiyar's burning desire to finish the English forces was more than palpable. Yielding to his suggestion, Syed Karki announced, 'My men have taken some grave losses while yours are still charged. Have them chase down the English if you so desire. But do return at the earliest for a debrief.'

'Time for payback!' Periya Maruthu Pandiyar snarled and quickly wrangled his men to go after the English.

The battle was over; the English were driven out. The battlefield was strewn with bodies of soldiers from both armies. The brown and green field had turned a deep shade of red in many places. The smell of burnt gunpowder was still in the air. The Mysuru cavalry returned after decimating the Arcot horses. But all was not finished for Syed Karki.

'Collect the wounded. Bring them into the city. Have the *hakims* treat them. Collect the muskets and bayonets and deposit them with the quartermasters. The bodies of the fallen enemies can be looted. You have my permission,' he instructed his men.

The Mysuru footmen split up to look for their wounded comrades and take them back to the city. They also rummaged through the dead bodies of their enemies and lightened the fallen of their valuables.

Velu Nachiyar was still with Syed Karki.

'This was a great victory,' she said somberly. 'We are just one step away from claiming Sivaganga back.'

'Yes, your highness. Let's strike the iron while it is. Let's proceed to Sivaganga and defeat the English once and for all.'

'I need to take care of something personal here, Syed. Let's stay here for a while. You could recoup some of your army's losses here while the wounded can heal themselves. I need to do something here in Kalayar Koil first, something that's important to me.'

The commander was a little confused, but he respected her decision.

'Sure, your highness. We can wait here until you are done with your work. We must wait for Periya Maruthu Pandiyar and his men anyway. I also need to work on replenishing our supplies.'

'Thank you, Commander Syed.'

Rani Velu Nachiyar and Syed Karki occupied some of the larger homes while the wounded were tended in the *mandapams* of the large temples in the town. Calm had returned to the town after the bloody battle.

Late one evening, Chinna Maruthu Pandiyar and Kuyili came into the main hall of the house where the queen was residing.

'We have found a local who can take us to the exact spot, my queen,' Chinna Maruthu Pandiyar began.

Velu Nachiyar immediately stood up. Her heart was racing.

'Let's go,' she said gingerly.

All three came out of the house. There was nobody outside.

'Where is he?'

'He has already pointed out the location to us, my queen. We will guide you there.'

'How are we going? On horseback?'

'No, my queen. We would need to walk to that place.'

As the three took the trail into the forest, Velu Nachiyar's heart was pounding, her mind was scrambled. She couldn't think straight. Her hands and legs were trembling. Her throat had gone dry. Following Kuyili and Chinna Maruthu Pandiyar seemed like a tedious task. She didn't keep track of where she was going. They had already entered the forest, but there was no trail. She merely followed the two. It got darker as the trees blocked out the rays from the setting sun. The walk seemed to take forever.

Finally, they stopped in the middle of the forest. The queen was too absorbed in her thoughts to notice.

In a low voice, Chinna Maruthu Pandiyar said, 'We are here.'

When Rani Velu Nachiyar eventually looked up, she realized they had paused inside the forest.

The general continued softly, 'This is the place where our king breathed his last, my queen. We don't know where the English took him afterwards.'

Velu Nachiyar didn't reply. She was visibly trembling.

Chinna Maruthu Pandiyar put his hand on Kuyili's shoulder.

'Let's go over there beyond those trees, Kuyili,' he said, guiding her along.

Kuyili, who was looking at her mother figure with wide eyes, quietly followed Chinna Maruthu Pandiyar.

The queen was now by herself. Staring at the ground, she steeled herself so she wouldn't burst into tears.

Then something gave way inside her, and she collapsed to her knees. Rani Velu Nachiyar succumbed to her grief, crying uncontrollably.

12

The onset of the summer of 1780, Kalayar Koil

'WE HAVE DEFEATED TWO MAJOR ARMIES. I WOULD PROPOSE we split into two groups, with the larger one heading to Sivaganga and the smaller crushing any remaining resistance in the kingdom.'

Syed Karki was surprised by the queen's proposal.

'Don't you think we should stay focused on the Sivaganga fort, your highness? The two major sources of trouble have been eliminated. I think we should put all our resources into reclaiming Sivaganga.'

'We are not yet out of the woods, Syed. There are still pockets of troublemakers in the kingdom. We need to weed them out as quickly as we can. We don't want them to become entrenched once we have taken over our kingdom and then fight a protracted battle. Nor do we want them to ambush us when we are in the vicinity of Sivaganga, trying to reclaim it. Also, doesn't your intelligence tell us that the garrison in the fort is small? We can surely afford to send some of our troops to clean up the last remnants of the enemy?'

Velu Nachiyar looked at the Maruthu brothers expectantly.

Both seemed to be utterly thrilled at the prospect of spreading their wings to take out multiple enemies at the same time.

'I agree with you, my queen. After successfully uprooting the two major obstacles on our way to Sivaganga, we must concentrate on covering a larger area and removing as many enemies as possible at the earliest. This will ensure a peaceful reign once you are back on the throne, my queen,' Chinna Maruthu Pandiyar argued.

Periya Maruthu Pandiyar put it more bluntly, 'I want to soak my sword in the blood of all those who stood against us. The sooner the better!'

Syed Karki was the only one who seemed concerned by this turn of events.

'Aren't we risking our chance of getting back Sivaganga by deploying a smaller force?' he asked in earnest.

The queen tried to assuage the commander's doubts.

'We will have our most capable soldiers engaged at Sivaganga fort. I too will be singularly invested in our operations at the fort. The entire body of Mysuru troops will be in Sivaganga with a singular objective – capturing the fort. All I am proposing is to send a small party under a capable general to clean out small pockets within the kingdom where our adversaries are holed up. This will protect us from any unpleasant surprises when we lay siege to Sivaganga. We will focus on a select few places where most of our adversaries are reposed. These places are not far from the main fort, and we can always call our troops back for assistance if the need arises.'

Commander Syed looked hard at Rani Velu Nachiyar.

The queen has been a tad nervous about dealing with the English, and her approach here goes against conventional military strategy. But she hasn't made a single wrong move in this campaign. I should go along with her proposal as it is her campaign, after all.

'Alright, your highness, we will go ahead with your proposal. What is the plan of action for the smaller group?'

'All lands south and west of Sivaganga are held by our allies. Mysuru holds all lands east of Sivaganga. It's only the northern lands that are not secure from our enemies. We need to capture Tirupattur. That will help us secure lands to the north and create a buffer zone against any enemy activity. A small contingent from our end should do the job. Chinna Pandi, I would like you to lead our troops and take back Tirupattur.'

'Yes, my queen,' the general replied. 'Tirupattur will be under your name in no time.'

Periya Maruthu Pandiyar felt left out.

'What about me, my queen?'

Smiling, she replied, 'I want you to clear out the path to Sivaganga by eliminating all our enemies along the way and keep us safe from any external threats during the siege. Make them pay dearly for all the misfortune they poured on us.'

With a grin on his face, Periya Maruthu Pandiyar responded, 'Of course, my queen!'

'We all have our tasks cut out. Now let's go and get back our kingdom!'

There was a chorus of confident approval from the attendees of the meeting at Kalayar Koil.

Over the next few days, Chinna Maruthu Pandiyar picked up supplies and, with a sizeable number of the Sivaganga troops, marched north towards Tirupattur. Once his younger brother left, Periya Maruthu Pandiyar picked his trusted men from the remaining Sivaganga army to start the march towards the Sivaganga fort. He led them out of Kalayar Koil to clear out an approach for Rani Velu Nachiyar. Syed Karki stayed put in Kalayar Koil along with the queen, awaiting replenishment of men and arms from Dindigul.

Even as the supplies arrived at Kalayar Koil over the next few weeks, Velu Nachiyar received word from Periya Maruthu Pandiyar that the way had been cleared and that he was waiting for them at a designated point. A pleasantly surprised rani headed to the commander's office.

The Dindigul commander was in discussion with his officers when Velu Nachiyar was ushered in by a retainer. Seeing the queen, Syed Karki dismissed his officers. He stood up from his desk to welcome her.

'Greetings, your highness. It is so good to see a smile on your face after all the hardships that you have encountered. Seeing you smile brings me joy.'

Graciously accepting the compliments, the queen began, 'Thank you, Commander Syed. There is good reason for all of us to be happy today. I just received a message from Peri Pandi. He has cleared the approach to Sivaganga. He said he barely faced any resistance on his way. He is presently scouting all places in the vicinity of the fort to clear any traces of enemy clans.'

'I don't think he is going to find much, your highness, and there is a good reason for that.'

Velu Nachiyar looked at Syed Karki with her eyes narrowed. Somehow, he always knew more about a situation than the rest in the group.

'And what is that?'

The commander went back to his desk and picked up a letter.

'The nawab of Mysuru has begun preparations to start a campaign against the English. He will be addressing the root of the problem itself by attacking Madras, the capital of the English. Since Arcot is on the way to Madras, the ruler of Arcot will be the first to face the wrath of the nawab of Myuru. I believe both the English and Arcot are withdrawing troops from the south and moving them up north to face our nawab. The field is now open for us here.'

Velu Nachiyar couldn't hide the excitement in her voice.

'This is indeed very promising news. Our path to Sivaganga has become a whole lot easier.'

But a look of concern soon clouded her face.

'Does that imply you need to take your troops up north to support Nawab Hyder Ali?'

'No, your highness,' Syed Karki reassured her. The troops promised by the nawab are still at your disposal.'

Pointing to the letter in his hand, he continued, 'In fact, the nawab has asked me to go ahead with our plan to attack the English at Sivaganga. He has more than enough numbers to sustain his campaign. Also, our attack here is akin to opening a new front in the campaign. We would also be pinning down a whole lot of English troops here who would have otherwise been sent north. So, vanquishing the English here would be beneficial for Mysuru.'

'It's good to hear that you will be with us till the end, Commander Syed. Do you plan to speed up our operations?'

'With the replenishments in place and the approach to Sivaganga cleared, we are good to go, your highness. Let's march to the rendezvous point suggested by your general.'

Soon, the army began marching out of Kalayar Koil.

As they approached Sivaganga, memories came rushing back to the queen.

It has been so many years since I last saw these gardens. They are filled with flowers, just as I remember. Their fragrance reminds me of my dear husband, with whom I used to frequent these gardens.

Walking around these ponds with my Muthu were some of the best moments of my life. And I lost it all ...

The happy memories soon gave way to a recollection of the tragedy that occurred at Kalayar Koil. Rani Velu Nachiyar's eyes welled up. But before the sorrow could drown her, the steely resolve to take back her kingdom firmed her up.

I will reclaim Sivaganga! I will not let you down, my love. I will get back our home!

The army junctioned with Periya Maruthu Pandiyar a few kilometres from the fort, beyond the visual range of the English garrison therein. A small but full-fledged camp had already been set up by the elder Maruthu general for the queen and the bulk of the army.

After an early dinner that evening, Periya Maruthu Pandiyar entered the queen's tent. Commander Syed was already inside. They were waiting for an update on the situation at the Sivaganga fort from the Sivaganga general.

'I am surprised by the situation around us, my queen. There was hardly anybody to stand up against us as we cleared the path to Sivaganga. My sword didn't get its fair share of English blood. I think everyone is holed up inside the fort. I am sure they know that we are here.'

Syed Karki responded, sounding a little distressed, 'Yes, they do. I think everybody is inside the fort. It's the safest place for them right now. There is no incentive for them to come out and face us. With an attack on Arcot and Madras imminent, I think the English have decided to stay put rather than risk it all. What do we do now?'

Velu Nachiyar was calm when she said, 'Let's see if they make any move.'

Before the monsoon of 1780, outside the Sivaganga fort

The weather was cool, the sky overcast. The rains were still a few weeks away. The camp that had been set up a few miles away from the Sivaganga fort was surprisingly quiet, except for the noise of the wind buffeting against the tent sidewalls. Over the course of these few months, wooden stockades had been set up and major communication lines of the English out of Sivaganga had been cut. But now, yet another impasse confronted them in their endeavour to recapture the city.

The rani was speaking in her usual sombre tone, 'I am extremely grateful to you and Nawab Hyder Ali for helping us come right up to the gates of my beloved Sivaganga. We have overcome many impossible obstacles. Crossing the gates of Sivaganga is the last of our hurdles. I request you again to attempt scaling the fort walls rather than camping here.'

'I do not desire anything more than seeing our swords dripping with English blood, your highness. But scaling the walls would be suicidal. We would lose everything that we have gained since the beginning of this operation. In the absence of siege equipment, and with the English troops, though diminished but well equipped with arms and ammunition, it will be a suicide mission.'

Velu Nachiyar remained silent. The commander of Dindigul continued, 'The English have been pinned down by Nawab Hyder Ali near Madras. Quite a few Arcot forts have been taken over by us. Our sources tell us that the English will not be sending any reinforcements to Sivaganga. I have already sent a letter requesting siege equipment. I am sure our nawab will accede to our request and grant us the necessary supplies. We just need to wait them to arrive before we make the final assault, your highness.'

The disappointment on Velu Nachiyar's face was palpable. Syed Karki didn't want to dishearten the queen.

'The only other way we can take the fort is if we fight the English out in the open, your highness. If we can lure them out, we will vanquish them in no time.'

He waited for the queen to respond to this proposition. But with no reply forthcoming, he started thinking of alternative approaches to capture the fort.

'We can even take the fight to the English once we are inside the fort. But for that, we need the gates to be opened for us. If we can open the gates of the fort, I promise you, Sivaganga will be yours.'

There was no change in the expression on the rani's face. Disappointment still wrought her face. She knew both options were unfeasible.

'We both know that both these options are next to impossible, Commander Syed. I guess we need to pursue the only viable option we have in hand right now. Let's wait for the siege equipment,' she said dejectedly.

'I only ask for your time and patience, your highness. We will have Sivaganga back. It's only a matter of time.'

The queen smiled but it didn't take away the disappointment from her face. Syed Karki didn't have anything more to convince her. He gave up. Resigned, he took leave. Velu Nachiyar closed her eyes.

So close, yet so far. How I wish I could be inside my home, my palace already. But I can't let the frustration at staying right outside the fort cloud my decisions. Syed is right. I can't risk the lives of my people with a momentary lapse of reason. I need to be patient. We have come a long way. I need to brace myself and wait for the equipment before mounting an attack.

Velu Nachiyar was still deep in her thoughts when Kuyili came inside the tent. Seeing her mother seated on the thick masand on the ground with her eyes closed, she stood still, waiting for her to open them.

The queen opened her eyes to find her daughter standing in front of her with a big smile on her face.

'What bothers you, Amma?' Kuyili asked sweetly.

Her infectious smile caught on with the rani.

'Come here, my child. Sit next to me. I was in talks with Syed Karki. We will not be able to breach Sivaganga without siege equipment. We need to wait for Mysuru to send the equipment before we mount an attack.'

'How long will that take, Amma?'

'Not long. They will be sending us the supplies soon, dear.'

'Why can't we just scale the walls? That will be quicker.'

'The English will shoot us down if we try that.'

'Is there no other way we can take back the fort?'

'Well, Syed Karki says if we get the gates of the fort open from the inside, we can proceed.'

Kuyili listened intently. She came out of the tent and walked to the makeshift stables. Picking a horse, she ambled her way to the Sivaganga fort. Her mind was completely focused on the discussion she had had with the queen.

As the fort appeared on the horizon, Kuyili stopped. She stared at the fort and saw some local women walking towards the fort gates.

Sivaganga troops had not laid a siege to the fort yet, but there was a blockade in place, which meant there was limited movement into and out of the fort. Kuyili was surprised on seeing the women walk towards the fort.

Why are they going to the fort? Would they be allowed inside?

She decided to find out and carefully galloped towards the women.

Back at the Sivaganga camp, Velu Nachiyar remained alone in her tent, even at dinner time. It was late by the time Kuyili returned. She had her usual infectious smile plastered on her face. Alighting from her horse, she ran to the queen's tent. The Udaiyal bodyguards outside the tent didn't stop their commander from entering the tent.

The queen was still sitting on her masand in a pensive state. Kuyili didn't offer any pleasantries to the queen and instead jumped straight to the point, 'Well, if Syed Sahib wants the gates open. We can do it for him.'

Rani Velu Nachiyar looked at Kuyili in surprise.

'How will you open the gates, Kuyili?'

'Vijayadashami is just a few days away. All the ladies from the nearby villages would be visiting the Raja Rajeshwari Amman temple inside the fort. The English, not wanting to antagonize the local populace, have decided to allow only women inside the fort on the day of Vijayadashami. We can blend in with the devotees and get inside. I will lead a small group of girls from our Udaiyal army and infiltrate the fort with concealed weapons. We will open the gates for you from the inside, Amma.'

Amazed at the speed with which Kuyili proposed the plan, Velu Nachiyar replied excitedly, 'This explains the heightened patrolling of the English on the ramparts of our Sivanganga fort these days. They have decided to allow civilians inside on account of Vijayadashami. But I think you just might have found a way around, my child. Let's run this idea by Peri Pandi and see if we can execute this plan.'

Hugging Kuyili, she continued, 'You raise the name of the Udaiyal army even higher, my daughter.'

An urgent meeting was called.

Periya Maruthu Pandiyar was elated.

'That's a brilliant idea, Kuyili. You are a smart girl!'

Kuyili, who was standing next to the seated queen, blushed at the compliment.

Syed Karki was still in doubt.

'Why would they allow villagers into the fort when they know we are outside?'

Rani Velu Nachiyar offered, 'This is a big festival, Commander Syed. It has been a tradition for hundreds of years.

Women from the neighbouring villages come to Sivaganga to celebrate this festival each year, no matter the circumstances. There will be a revolt inside the fort if the English don't allow this practice for any reason.'

Periya Maruthu Pandiyar added, 'They may not open the large gate, but why wouldn't they open the small gate for the local people? This is a much safer option for them, as it can allow only one passage at a time, especially when surrounded by a hostile force. They can control who gets inside the fort this way. Also, we have been sitting idle for months now. I don't think the English will expect us to attack them after all this time.'

Syed Karki swayed in the direction of Kuyili's proposal. Going with the flow, he asked, 'If they are going to allow civilians, we need to get our people inside. So, what is the plan?'

Velu Nachiyar looked at Kuyili. Taking cue from her queen, she responded, 'I would move the best of the Udaiyal soldiers to a village nearby. From there, we will proceed towards Sivaganga on the day of Vijayadashami. We will hide our aruvals in baskets filled with flowers. Once we enter the fort, our objective would be to open the gates and signal the troops from the ramparts.'

'Your plan sounds simple and logical, Kuyili, but we all know things can change upon first contact with the enemy. The English are sure to be more cautious during this period. We need to plan for contingencies.'

Kuyili didn't want to get into the what-ifs of the operation.

'Syed Sahib, I will open the gates for you,' she said resolutely. 'I promise you. You don't need to worry about a thing.'

Kuyili's resolve seemed to influence the Dindigul commander as well.

The risks of a failed infiltration are minimal, but the rewards are substantial. I like the girl's confidence. We should go ahead with this plan.

'Alright, Kuyili. I will be waiting for you to open the gates.'

With everyone in consensus, Periya Maruthu Pandiyar declared, 'Good! Kuyili, come with me. I will give you all the details about the layout of the fort that you'll need for the operation. We have intelligence reports on the possible sentry locations. Let's work around those as well. We have lots of planning to do now, so let's go.'

The Udaiyal commander prepared a small crack team from her army to infiltrate the fort. With Vijayadashami just a few days away, the group disguised themselves as villagers and moved to a village that was loyal to the queen.

Vijayadashami, the last of the ten-day celebration of the victory of good over evil, arrived. From late afternoon, there was a steady stream of women from the surrounding villages entering Sivaganga. Many of them carried baskets of flowers, clothes, fruits and earthen lamps on their heads. Some carried betel leaves in smaller baskets while others held containers filled with ghee and other oils. A few women brought their cows and other smaller livestock along with them. There was a festive spirit that imbued these women, who were completely oblivious to the impending danger right outside the fort. Security at the gate of the fort was more vigilant than in previous years. The sepoys at the gate were frisking each and every person entering the fort. The heightened security caused some heated exchanges of words between the local populace entering the fort and the sepoys guarding the gate.

Kuyili and her soldiers blended themselves with the local ladies to minimize the risk of getting caught. Their plan was to regroup behind the Raja Rajeshwari Amman temple before the main pooja in the evening began.

Kuyili was carrying a big basket of flowers on her head. She was dressed in a red saree, with her thick black hair neatly knotted behind her head. Her almond-shaped, dusky face was lit up with a bright smile. Nearing the gate, she saw the sepoys rummaging through each of the baskets that were being carried by the women ahead of her. The delays caused by these overt security measures seemed to have agitated the villagers, who were vociferously demanding the sepoys let them inside.

'Move on already! The pooja will start soon!'

The harried sepoys ignored the angry protestations and continued with their job. Soon, it was Kuyili's turn.

The sepoy ordered Kuyili, 'Keep your basket down!'

He started removing the flowers in a haphazard manner. An old lady standing right behind Kuyili yelled at the sepoy, 'What's wrong with you? The flowers have been tied delicately. It is an offering to Amman. Do you want to be cursed for your vile actions?'

The fear of God took over the sepoy. He placed the flowers back in the basket.

'Alright, you are cleared! Get in!'

Even for a short-statured girl like Kuyili, this small entry door was too tiny. She gently bent down to get inside and proceeded towards the temple along with the other women. There were bright banners all around. Colourful rangolis had been drawn on the floor around the temple. Kuyili moved along the outer walls until she reached a spot behind the temple, where a few of her girls were already waiting.

'Let's wait for the rest to come in. How many were guarding the door?'

'Not many, just a handful,' one of the girls replied.

'We won't start until the pooja has begun and the doors of the fort are closed. Ensure that you identify the path to the ramparts and eliminate everyone guarding the doors. Take out your weapons and hide them under your clothes,' she instructed her army of women warriors who nodded in agreement.

In the next hour or so, every one of the Udaiyal soldiers had made it inside and assembled behind the temple. With everyone inside, Kuyili spoke, 'Now we head inside the temple for the pooja. When I stand up and start heading to the back of the temple, all of you start moving one by one. Do not start together and don't do anything that could arouse suspicion. I will give out the next set of instructions once we assemble here again later in the night. Until then, mingle with the ladies and take part in the festivities. Keep an eye on your surroundings.'

With these instructions, the Udaiyal soldiers dispersed and waited for the signal from Kuyili.

The festivities were deliberately kept low-key by the English due to the threat of Rani Velu Nachiyar outside the fort, but the big festival at night was to go ahead as planned. All the ladies had congregated at the main temple. As the sun set, the religious rituals began in earnest. The entire fort brightened up, with fire torches lighting every nook and cranny of the temple. Some of the sepoys too made their way to the temple to partake in the celebration.

At the assigned hour, Kuyili stood up and proceeded to the back of the temple with her basket. Seeing her move, the

Udaiyal soldiers too got up, one at a time, and moved to the rear of the temple.

Once all the soldiers had clandestinely congregated, Kuyili began, 'Let's split into two groups and approach the gates of the fort from two sides. Eliminate anyone who is in your way. But do it quietly and don't raise any alarms. Once you reach the gates, take out all the sentries. Break the locks and then, whoever is closest to the ramparts, climb up, light the fire torch and signal the scouts waiting outside. Keep yourself undercover at all times.'

The soldiers took out their aruvals and split into two groups, each moving in opposite directions. Kuyili was with the first group. The warriors started moving carefully, keeping to the spots untouched by the fire torches. As they moved out of the temple premises, Kuyili saw a large single-storeyed rectangular building further behind the temple with a sizeable number of sepoys guarding it.

The whitewashed building, with a small door as its only entry point, looked well guarded. Suddenly, something dawned on Kuyili.

This must be the ammunition depot for the English! Syed sahib has been talking about the arsenal of the English. No wonder they were so keen on staying inside the fort! They want to safeguard the ammunition. It needs to be taken out. Destroying their ammunition depot will cripple the English.'

She ordered the soldiers with her to stop. There was a change in plan.

'You girls go ahead. I will head to the ammunition depot over there and destroy it. Ensure that you break the locks and send out the signal as planned.'

The soldiers accepted the orders of their leader and moved ahead.

The window of opportunity to take out the ammunition depot was closing fast.

What do I do? How do I take out the depot?

Kuyili looked around and found some paraphernalia kept against one side of the outer wall of the temple. Walking over to that place, she saw a bunch of pooja supplies – flowers, fruits, betel leaves, turmeric and more. Sitting close to the wall was a metal cauldron. Kuyili peered inside the cauldron.

Ghee!

The cauldron was filled to the brim with ghee. It was to be used for the deity later in the night. Kuyili's mind started racing.

Without further ado, she picked the cauldron and poured all the ghee over herself. The grease dripped from her body down to the ground, making her look like a goddess who had been purified before the big pooja. Kuyili wiped off the ghee from her eyes. She removed a torch from the wall of the temple, grabbing it in her left hand and, with her aruval in her right one, charged towards the depot.

Like an incarnation of Raja Rajeshwari Amman, Kuyili raced towards the depot with a vengeance. It was an extraordinary sight to behold. The sepoys standing guard stood petrified, taking her to be the mother goddess herself who had manifested to burn them down.

Kuyili slashed two sepoys at the front with her aruval. They both collapsed into a pool of their own blood.

The door to the depot was unlocked. Even as Kuyili opened it, two more sepoys came from behind. Fending them off with the fire torch, she lunged at one of them, slashing his neck and quickly moved to stab the second one to death. More sepoys started running towards her. Time was of the essence. She quickly turned around and entered the depot.

Upon entering, Kuyili found the depot filled with barrels packed with gunpowder and saltpetre. There were a multitude of other arms as well.

This has to be destroyed!

Not wasting a moment, she touched the fire torch to herself. Her saree, soaked with ghee, quickly caught fire. Upon seeing Kuyili ablaze, the sepoys ran back out for their lives. With a smile on her face, Kuyili jumped on the gunpowder tumbrils.

Rani Velu Nachiyar and her army had moved closer to the fort but were still out of sight of any sentries in the Sivaganga fort. Hiding amongst the thick, dry bushes, the Kuzzaks were at the vanguard of the column ready to make a quick charge once the gates opened. The queen and Syed Karki were with the cavalry in order to lead the charge, and the Sivaganga soldiers were right behind the horses. Since most of the leaders of the Sivaganga army knew the layout of the city and the fort, they were to secure the main palace once the cavalry captured the gates of the fort. The slower-moving Mysuru infantry made up the rear of the column. They were to support the rest in case of any exigencies. The entire army was hiding in silence. Even the generally boisterous Sivaganga men and women were in a tense silence waiting for the signal from their scouts to mount an attack. All of a sudden, there was a huge explosion inside the fort. The army was startled but they held steady in their positions. Nobody knew what had happened. The fire in the fort could be seen spreading from afar.

A concerned rani asked, 'What happened?'

The ever-calm commander was also a little shaken by the detonation.

'Such a big explosion is out of the ordinary. My guess is that their ammunition has been blown up. We'll have to wait for news from our scouts, your highness.'

The blast shook the women warriors inside the fort. But they didn't waver and continued towards the gate. The sepoys manning the ramparts ran towards the site of the explosion, leaving the gates unchecked for the Udaiyal soldiers. Within a few minutes, the locks were broken and the gates of the fort were opened. With the flames engulfing the place, the warriors realized a fire torch signal would be difficult to identify.

They raced to the horses by the gate and mounted them. As the horses galloped out, the remaining Udaiyal soldiers stood guard at the gate, ensuring it remained open.

The cavalry scouts of Mysuru, who were waiting outside the fort, saw the horses running out with some Udaiyal soldiers atop them.

The women warriors were shouting, 'The gates are open! The gates are open for us! We need to get in!'

The cavalry scouts and the Udaiyal soldiers galloped to the main army and headed straight towards the queen.

'The gates have been opened, my queen,' one of the soldiers

called out. 'The rest of my comrades are guarding the gate. We need to enter now.'

'What was that explosion?'

'I think the ammunition depot of the English has been blown up.'

'Good, my child! Where is Kuyili?'

The Udaiyal women lowered their heads.

'We don't know, my queen. Our commander ordered us to go open the gates while she herself went to the ammunition depot.'

Velu Nachiyar feared the worst. The thought of losing Kuyili singed her. She sat stunned on her horse.

My daughter …

With time running out, Syed Karki came forward to the queen.

'I am praying for the survival of Kuyili, your highness. But now it is time to attack. The English have lost their ammunition and the gates are open. We need to take the fort, this is our moment. We are awaiting your orders.'

The queen regained her composure. Nodding in agreement, she declared, 'Forward! Forward for Udaiyal! Forward for Kuyili!'

As the fire spread inside the fort, the Mysuru cavalry surged forward towards the open gates of Sivaganga in a column formation.

There were no sepoys inside the gates. The cavalry joined the Udaiyal guards at the gate and waited for the infantry to join them. Commander Syed and the rani soon followed with the infantry in tow.

Taking it all in, Syed Karki announced, 'The English must have grouped for a last stand somewhere in the middle, your highness. Let's deploy our infantry and finish them off.'

Velu Nachiyar agreed.

Syed Karki ordered the officer in charge of the infantry, 'Comb the area. The English must be preparing for a last stand somewhere inside. Signal us once you find them.'

With the commander's order, the troops flooded the streets, looking for English sepoys. A few that were found were promptly bayoneted by the Mysuru foot soldiers, but no large groups of English troops were to be seen. Syed Karki now moved with his bodyguards and the cavalry to the location of the explosion. Meanwhile, Velu Nachiyar headed towards the palace with the remainder of the cavalry and her Udaiyal bodyguards.

Upon arriving at the site of the explosion, Syed Karki found bodies strewn all over the place. The roof of the ammunition depot was completely blown. He addressed his officer, 'The explosion seems to have killed most of the English soldiers. But we need to be sure. Search the entire area and eliminate any remaining sepoys. Rescue all surviving civilians.'

The cavalry went scouring for enemies while Syed Karki remained at the site of the explosion, taking stock of the situation.

Velu Nachiyar reached the palace accompanied by the cavalry. It looked just as it had the day she left Sivaganga. There was no one around to stop her, and an eerie calm engulfed the place. Her soldiers had already taken control of the palace and sanitized it of any adversaries before the queen could enter. Rani Velu Nachiyar, still on her horse, looked up to see an Udaiyal soldier scaling the palace's tall spire to tear down the English flag and replace it with the flag of Sivaganga.

13

Before the monsoon of 1780, the Sivaganga palace

RANI VELU NACHIYAR WAS WEARING A RED SILK SAREE VERY similar to the one she had worn while escaping Kollangudi. Decked in the royal jewellery safeguarded by the priestly class all these years, she looked considerably older but still had a regal air while seated on the throne. A rejuvenated Vellachi sat by her side.

The Maruthu brothers and Syed Karki were in their ceremonial military garb and stood in the durbar hall along with the other generals.

The rani announced, 'We have finally reclaimed our home. The hardships we faced in the last eight years have come to an end at last. Numerous men and women have made the ultimate sacrifice to make this day a reality. We will never forget them; they will live forever in our hearts.'

Her eyes welled up as she continued speaking.

'I will perform my daughter Kuyili's last rites at Pasangarai, the home of her ancestors. I'll have a *veer kal*, a hero's stone, installed there and a temple built in her honour. Her heroic act helped us take back Sivaganga from the English. She will henceforth be called Veera Mahakali Thee Paayndha Amman, the brave woman who plunged into the arsenal with fire.'

There was an applause of appreciation from the people in the durbar.

'I will also perform the last rites of my loyal bodyguard Udaiyal in Kollangudi and instal a Veer Kal there and build a temple in her honour. She will henceforth be known as Vettu Udaiyal Kali Amman, the brave woman, who despite injuries, never left the side of dharma and saved her queen.'

Taking off her diamond-studded mangalyam, she continued, 'I would like to offer this mangalyam as the first donation towards the construction and consecration of the temple in Kollangudi.'

Applause reverberated through the walls of the durbar.

'The king of Sivaganga's last rites never took place,' she continued, as the applause died down. 'I would like to bring closure to my loving husband in Kalayar Koil.'

Wiping away her tears, she looked at the Maruthu brothers and smiled.

'We would have never come close to Sivaganga, let alone taken it back, if it wasn't for the valiant actions of the Maruthu brothers. They stood like rocks by my side through thick and thin. They inspired the citizenry to take up arms against our adversaries and led them with courage to defeat our enemies on the battlefield. I will always be grateful for their heroic deeds and unflinching loyalty.'

The Maruthu brothers bowed in gratitude.

The queen continued, 'I hereby appoint Periya Maruthu Pandiyar as the commander-in-chief of the Sivaganga army and Chinna Maruthu Pandiyar as the prime minister of Sivaganga.'

There was a thunderous ovation in the hall, and everyone congratulated the Maruthu brothers on their appointment.

Once the clapping simmered down, the queen of Sivaganga looked at Syed Karki.

'The assistance offered to us by Nawab Hyder Ali and his able commander, Syed Karki, has been invaluable and we are perpetually indebted to them for all their help. We will forever remain allies of and friends with the Mysuru kingdom, and we will not hesitate for a second if they ever seek our support. Thank you, Commander Karki, for your enormous aid in helping us recover our home. Please convey my gratitude to the nawab of Mysuru.'

Syed Karki bowed before the queen.

'I will convey your message to our nawab, your highness,' he replied. 'He will no doubt be delighted to hear that the reins of Sivaganga are back in the right hands.'

'As a token of appreciation, I will build a mosque and church in Sivaganga,' the queen resumed. 'These buildings will be a symbol of the friendship between Sivaganga and Mysuru. Your soldiers and officers are more than welcome to pay a visit.'

'Thank you, your highness,' the commander bowed again, placing a hand on his chest.

'This has been a long and hard campaign. I would urge you to spend some time here as our state guest and recuperate yourself. I also request your assistance in strengthening and modernizing the army of Sivaganga through ways of training and discipline.'

'I am honoured by your kind gesture, your highness. But Mysuru is still in the midst of a war with the English. Mappila Thevar, the uncle of the imprisoned king of Ramanathapuram,

Muthuramalinga Sethupathi, has requested assistance from our nawab to relieve their kingdom from the clutches of Arcot and the English. The nawab has asked me to proceed to Ramanathapuram and drive out our enemies. In my absence, I would recommend you utilize the services of my French general, Duprès. He can help you modernize your army credibly.'

'I understand, Syed Karki. Your duty calls. We will definitely utilize the services of General Duprès. I thank you again for your efforts.'

She signalled to her courtier, who soon arrived with the finest of silks and gold jewellery.

'Please accept these small gifts. I pray that we see you again in the near future.'

Syed Karki bowed again and exited the durbar.

Velu Nachiyar now addressed the people of her kingdom. 'My people have suffered far too long. The explosion at the fort, though impactful, has caused significant damage to many buildings in the vicinity. The infrastructure has suffered as well since the time we were driven out of our homeland. All the money from the treasury has been drained by the Arcot prince. I need to provide succour to my people. I need to rebuild Sivaganga to its past glory.'

Standing up from her throne, the queen announced, 'As a first task, I would like to renovate all the temples in the kingdom that have suffered damage. I will begin this exercise by renovating the temple of the royal deity Raja Rajeshwari Amman here in the capital.'

Turning to Chinna Maruthu Pandiyar, she said, 'You have successfully captured Tirupattur. I urge you to head there to set up a base. Please undertake any actions you deem necessary to improve the area's economy and renovate the temples that have been damaged. I will focus my energies on the capital in the interim.'

Chinna Maruthu Pandiyar nodded in agreement.

Periya Maruthu Pandiyar interjected, 'I would request the opportunity to get the temple in Kalayar Koil renovated, my queen. It is my desire to build the tallest of gopurams for this temple.'

'Please go ahead, Peri Pandi. Use Kalayar Koil as your base for the improvement of the larger region.'

Concluding the durbar session, the rani announced, 'From here on, Dussehra will be celebrated with great pomp and grandeur. For it was on the day of Vijayadashami that Sivaganga was liberated. Starting now, all temples will receive donations from the state during this festival.'

For the next few years, the queen of Sivaganga went about strengthening the infrastructure, economy and military of the kingdom. The coffers slowly started filling up again and the country stabilized.

Vellachi's long absence from urban civilization meant that she didn't have the mental acumen to take on royal duties with ease. Velu Nachiyar brought in tutors to prepare her daughter for the tasks of the court. Although she was responding well to her treatment back home, the recurrent relapses meant that Vellachi spent most of her time with her doctors than tutors and barely focussed on her royal duties.

The ravages of time and guerrilla warfare started taking their toll on Rani Velu Nachiyar's health. She started suffering from a heart ailment. Accepting her slowly deteriorating health,

Velu Nachiyar began focusing on religious matters while the Maruthu brothers took over the administration, military and economy of the kingdom. Their popularity among the local populace grew by the day, while the queen steadily slipped into the background. The Maruthu brothers became the de facto leaders of Sivaganga, beloved by its citizens.

The winter of 1784, the Sivaganga palace

Chinna Maruthu Pandiyar was in an agitated state, while his older brother was seething with anger. The only other person in the durbar, Rani Velu Nachiyar, was in her usual calm demeanour.

'This is the best course of action, Chinna Pandi,' she was saying.

'No, my queen!' the new prime minister was saying. 'We should not be paying a single rupee to that scoundrel, Wallajah. He has no right to ask us for a tribute.'

Periya Maruthu Pandiyar spoke in an even more aggressive tone: 'We should be fighting the Arcot soldiers for all that they have done to us. My army is now stronger than ever, thanks to the training and battle tactics taught by General Duprès. We should be going to war against Arcot rather than submitting ourselves to become their feudatory!'

Velu Nachiyar tried to calm the situation.

'The war between the English and Mysuru is coming to an end. Both are suing for peace. The Arcot army, though diminished in strength, still stands strong. It has been two years since our source of strength, Nawab Hyder Ali, passed away. His son Tipu Sultan has been cordial, but we still don't know his intentions for Arcot. However, everyone is seeking peace now. As should we.'

'Seek peace by becoming a feudatory state! We have never submitted ourselves to Arcot, and we never will. Our army can serve a befitting reply to any aggression initiated by the Arcot nawab,' the commander-in-chief bellowed.

'I have all the confidence in you and our army's capability, Peri Pandi. But I yearn for peace. This is an opportunity for lasting peace. The nawab of Arcot has even reduced the amount of the annual tribute he seeks. He is now asking for one lakh and seventy-five thousand rupees. This may still be a small fortune, but paying it will help us retain our freedom and control over the future of Sivaganga. We will not have to anticipate any more attacks from Arcot or the English.'

Chinna Maruthu Pandiyar shook his head in disagreement. He replied, 'This is all an elaborate scheme plotted by Wallajah to bring back the Marava lands under his control. He released Muthuramalinga Sethupathi, the king of Ramanathapuram, within a few months after we had retrieved Sivaganga four years ago. The only condition for release was a reduced annual tribute and a pledge of allegiance to the nawab. He is trying to pull the same trick on us. Wallajah is trying to circumvent the hard-fought freedom we gained and bring us back into his fold.'

'My cousin Muthuramalinga Sethupathi has been running Ramanathapuram as an independent kingdom, and the annual tribute is merely an overhead expenditure for him. There is peace in the neighbouring Marava country, and I seek the same peace here,' the queen said determinedly.

'The king of Ramanathapuram is a stooge of Wallajah, and I wouldn't like to see you like that, my queen,' Chinna Maruthu Pandiyar replied.

'We cannot be on a war-path forever, Chinna Pandi. For our kingdom to survive and thrive, we need long periods of peace, and today I see an opportunity for such peace.'

The Maruthu brothers were not convinced.

But the queen didn't give up.

'My husband never denied Arcot's right to seek a tribute from us. I don't want to break the promise made by the late king to the nawab.'

Periya Maruthu Pandiyar immediately interjected, 'Yet, they murdered our king in deception! How can we trust the Arcot nawab will not do the same again?'

Rani Velu Nachiyar tried to reason with the Maruthu brothers one last time, 'Consider this the request of an old woman. You have trusted my judgement for so many years. I urge you to trust me on this decision as well. It is for the greater good of the kingdom.'

The Maruthu brothers remained silent.

'I will write a letter to Wallajah accepting his offer for a reduced tribute and extract a promise of no future aggression between the two kingdoms.'

With the last word, the rani left the durbar.

Chinna Maruthu Pandiyar looked at his elder brother and said, 'Our queen has never taken any decision without consensus. She has changed. Old age and poor health change a person; they make one rigid. With every passing year, our queen is becoming more obstinate.'

'She has not been the same since we took back Sivaganga,' Periya Maruthu Pandiyar replied. 'She is spending more and more time in religious activities than administration. She has lost her innately martial nature, which came to our rescue while we were in exile.'

'Even though I don't agree with her decision, she is still our queen, and we need to respect her decision.'

'But if her age is impairing her decision-making capability, then we need to do something, Chinna Pandi.'

'Yes, not today, though.'

'So what do we do now?'

'Let's go ahead with our queen's decision, Peri Pandi. We can even pay the first tranche of the tribute. Since I control the treasury, I will make sure that not another rupee goes out to Wallajah after this.'

Summer of 1788, the Sivaganga palace

The durbar was filled with nobles and aristocrats with the rani at the helm.

'As many of you are aware, I have been suffering from a heart ailment since the last few years,' the queen of Sivaganga was saying. 'I will not be with you all for long, and we need a succession plan to ensure the longevity of the kingdom. To that end, I would like to announce with pride that I have decided to adopt a close relative from my late husband's side of the family, Gowri Vallabha Thevar. The boy is bright, astute and has the strength to take our kingdom to the next level.'

Everyone applauded the announcement, except for the Maruthu brothers, who remained silent with a stoic look plastered on their faces.

The young man was brought forward to the raised platform. Rani Velu Nachiyar put her hands on the boy's shoulders and said, 'I trust you will show the same support, devotion and loyalty to this boy as you have to me.'

Later that evening, the Maruthu brothers were in the queen's personal quarters.

'We have always envisaged Vellachi as the next ruler of Sivaganga, my queen', Chinna Maruthu Pandiyar said. 'Today's decision goes contrary to our expectations.'

'Vellachi is physically and mentally not up to the mark when it comes to the rigours of running a kingdom. Due to our unfortunate circumstances, she was forced to grow up in the forests where she lacked proper education and physical training. Having her as the next ruler will not be a prudent decision. Gowri Vallabha Thevar, on the other hand, is educated and well trained. He has the acumen and capacity to lead the state. Even though, I may not be the biological mother of the boy, I am sure the kingdom will see better days under his leadership.'

'Well, we can't punish Vellachi for circumstances beyond her control. We are taking away what rightfully belongs to her.'

'It is in the best interest of the state to have Gowri Vallabha Thevar rather than Vellachi as the next ruler, Chinna Pandi.

I love my daughter, but sadly, I haven't been a good mother to her and it's my fault that today she is not in a position to take over the reins of the kingdom. I don't want to further my mistake by staking the future of Sivaganga on her weak shoulders.'

'We are here to guide Vellachi in the right direction, my queen.'

'Gowri would be an asset, while Vellachi would slow you down, Chinna Pandi. The most competent person at the helm will the best thing for you and Peri Pandi.'

'But you are not doing justice to your daughter. This is not fair!'

'I understand your concern. This may not seem fair, but this is the right thing to do.'

'I don't think so, my queen.'

Rani Velu Nachiyar remained silent.

Periya Maruthu Pandiyar concluded the interaction by saying, 'We too know what's best for the kingdom.'

Without waiting for a reply or dismissal, the Maruthu brothers left the queen's quarters.

'The queen has finally lost her bearings. There is no rationality in her decisions,' Periya Maruthu Pandiyar said upon entering his younger brother's house.

'The very existence of our kingdom is at stake now. I don't trust the boy, Peri Pandi. He will never understand the struggles we went through to get here. He may follow in the footsteps of our queen and hand over the kingdom on a platter to Arcot,' Chinna Maruthu Pandiyar fumed.

'We need to do something before it's too late.'

'We need to remove the queen's loyalists from all civil and military posts. Once we enlist our men in these positions, it would be difficult for the queen to implement her irrational decisions.'

'That's a good idea. Let's start immediately, Chinna Pandi.'

A few weeks later, a courtier entered the rani's personal quarters and announced, 'Another batch of military officers have arrived seeking refuge, my queen.'

Velu Nachiyar got up from her bed.

'Provide them with lodging and all other amenities. No one should be turned back,' she instructed.

'Yes, my queen. The leader of this contingent requests a meeting with you. He says he has important information for you.'

Velu Nachiyar ordered for him to be sent in.

A few minutes later, a military officer entered the room.

He began, 'The Maruthu brothers have mounted an aggressive campaign to remove and replace all officers and civil servants who are loyal to you, my queen. Our commander-in-chief, Periya Maruthu Pandiyar, doesn't even hesitate to deploy the army to force out people who refuse his directives. Prime Minister Chinna Maruthu Pandiyar has cut off funds to anyone who still stands by your side. They are systematically removing your influence over the kingdom, my queen.'

'Yes, I'm aware,' the queen added, somewhat defeatedly.

'We must do something, my queen. This is tantamount to a coup!'

The queen remained silent, lost in her thoughts.

The Maruthu brothers have been upset with my decisions over the last few years and I've to make them see my point of view. The kingdom's purse strings and administrative powers are in their hands. Now they're taking over every last matter, too. Over the last decade, since we got the reins of our kingdom back, the Maruthu brothers have proven their worth, time and again. They are dependable and hold a lot of sway over the people and politics of our state. There is little I can do without escalating things and agitating my people. The people of Sivaganga love me, but they love the brothers equally. Any adverse action from my side will only precipitate things to a point of no return. I am walking on eggshells here.

Coming out of her reverie, the queen began, 'I have sent them multiple messages, but they are yet to meet me in person. Their reply is the same every time – that they're busy with reorganization.'

'They are filling up all the posts with their loyalists, my queen. They are sidelining you and are on the verge of taking control of the kingdom. They might very well mount a similar campaign here at Sivaganga fort too.'

'Our fort is a safe haven. If they really wanted to harm me, they would have done that a long time back – they control the army after all. I still believe that they have respect and love for me. You will be safe here, officer. The Maruthu brothers would never attack me or any of our people. If anyone needs safety and security, you may ask them to come here.'

'Yes, my queen,' the contingent leader bowed and left.

A courtier entered the room.

'A messenger from the Arcot nawab arrived this morning and has delivered this message, my queen.'

Handing over a letter to Velu Nachiyar, the courtier stood at the door, awaiting further instructions. Reading the letter put the rani on edge.

Oh no! Wallajah has got wind of the situation here. He says he will be sending troops to support my cause and Gowri Vallabha Thevar's adoption. The Arcot nawab still sees the Maruthu brothers as a threat. They have reinforced that feeling in the nawab by not paying the promised annual tribute. Wallajah is trying to undermine the Maruthu brothers under the guise of helping me. I need to stop him before this escalates!

The queen quickly got to her writing table and began drafting a letter. Thanking the nawab for his offer, she refused his help. She emphasized that this was an internal matter of Sivaganga that she would deal with in her own capacity and requested Wallajah to withdraw his troops.

Handing over the letter to the courtier, she instructed him, 'Hurry up and ensure that the letter reaches the nawab of Arcot at the earliest.'

A few days later, the commander-in-chief's spies arrived at his camp.

'The Arcot nawab's army has reached the borders of Tirupattur,' one of the spies informed him. 'They will soon overwhelm our base there.'

'Direct all my troops to Tirupattur,' Periya Maruthu Pandiyar roared. 'Every sword should be directed towards Wallajah.'

The Sivaganga troops paused all current campaigns and began their march towards Tirupattur. By the time they reached, the nawab's troops had overrun the place. The

Sivaganga soldiers who knew the terrain, rapidly routed their enemies and had on them on the retreat. Tirupattur was taken back as quickly as it was lost.

The prime minister, who was forcing out the queen's civil servants near Sivaganga, joined his elder brother at Tirupattur. Taking stock of the situation, he said, 'The nerve of Wallajah to attack us on our own territory! We need to make him pay for his transgressions. Let's march into his land and ravage everything he values. We need to teach him a lesson he never forgets.'

The relieving forces changed directions and marched into Arcot, burning everything and anything that offered resistance. After a few days of plunder, Periya Maruthu Pandiyar, convinced that the brutal message had been conveyed to the Arcot nawab, directed his troops back to Kollangudi.

But the actions of the Maruthu brothers had the opposite effect on Wallajah. Seeking retribution, the nawab sought the assistance of the English in Madras. Soon, a contingent led by Colonel James Stuart, along with the troops from Tondaiman of Pudukkottai, began their march to Kollangudi. The English also managed to lure away General Duprès from Sivaganga and extract invaluable information about the terrain from him, which enabled them to reach Kollangudi in a much shorter time, without encountering any scouts of the Sivaganga army.

Unperturbed by the sudden appearance of English troops, the Sivaganga army faced the challenge head-on. But the superior troops of the English were able to overcome the fight offered to them and push the soldiers out of Kollangudi. Periya

Maruthu Pandiyar ordered his troops to head over to Kalayar Koil, where, with better defences in place, it would be easier to pin down the enemy forces.

Before things could escalate any further, Rani Velu Nachiyar sent letters to Wallajah and the English through her diplomatic channels. The queen still held a good standing in the courts of Arcot and the offices of the English. Her letters, seeking a de-escalation, were honoured, and the English and Arcot withdrew their troops from Sivaganga. An unsteady peace now existed in the kingdom.

The Maruthu brothers were at their base in Kalayar Koil.

Chinna Maruthu Pandiyar began, 'Our enemies attacked us in response to our actions in Arcot. But I hear the motivation behind the initial movement of Arcot soldiers into Tirupattur was in the spirit of supporting the queen against us.'

'My spies also informed me that the English support Gowri Vallabha Thevar as the successor of the queen, Chinna Pandi. So, they readily accepted Wallajah's request to attack us.'

'Something is afoot between the queen and the English.'

'It was the queen's word that made them retreat too. There is surely something happening in the shadows.'

'I don't know, Peri Pandi. But what I do know is that if the queen remains at the helm, Sivaganga will lose its independence.'

'I think she has already pledged our freedom to the English.'

'We are on our own now.'

14

The winter of 1790, the Sivaganga palace

THE RIFT BETWEEN RANI VELU NACHIYAR AND THE MARUTHU brothers only widened after her diplomatic success with the English and Arcot. The upset Maruthu brothers stopped coming to the Sivaganga fort and all communication gradually dwindled.

There was a precarious peace on the borders of the kingdom, with a cold war brewing on the inside. So when the Maruthu brothers suddenly sought an appointment with the queen, it came as a surprise to her. Fearing the worst, Velu Nachiyar granted them an immediate appointment.

The queen was seated on her throne in the durbar when the Maruthu brothers entered the hall. There was no love lost between them, but the brothers still accorded respect to their queen by bowing before her.

The prime minister said, 'We came to know that Muthuramalinga Sethupathi, the ruler of Ramanathapuram, has sought the hand of Princess Vellachi.'

'Yes, Chinna Pandi. With Vellachi coming of age, we received a formal proposal of marriage from the ruler of Ramanathapuram.'

'I strongly protest this alliance, my queen. That man is a stooge of the Arcot nawab. He owes his place on the throne to Wallajah. His intentions are sinister, and he seeks to usurp our beloved Sivaganga on behalf of Arcot with this marriage.'

'I thought Muthuramalinga Sethupathi doesn't pay the annual tribute to Wallajah, just like us. How would that make him a stooge of Arcot?'

'Yes, he doesn't, but at the same time he instigates the nawab against us by stating that his decision is based on our refusal to pay the annual tribute.'

Velu Nachiyar smiled at her protégé. Even though she had agreed to pay the annual tribute, her prime minister had refused to release the money to Arcot. It was the Maruthu brothers' aggression a year back that had led them into battle against the English and Arcot. A mere statement by the ruler of Ramanathapuram would hardly provoke the Arcot nawab. But all of this was water under the bridge, and she didn't counter Chinna Maruthu Pandiyar's argument.

'Yes, Chinna Pandi. I don't trust Muthuramalinga Sethupathi's intentions, but an alliance between the two Marava countries is the need of the hour. What do you suggest?'

Periya Maruthu Pandiyar, who had been standing silently until then, replied, 'It's not just about political alliance. We need a suitable partner for our princess. If the aim is to strengthen our alliance with Ramanathapuram, then I would suggest a relative from your mother's side, Vengan Udaya Thevar. He would be a suitable match for our princess and would also rebuild the alliance between the two countries.'

This is a good opportunity to rebuild the bridges with Peri Pandi and Chinna Pandi. It's good that they don't trust Muthuramalinga Sethupathi. I, too, have my doubts about him. I don't have a high opinion of Vengan Udaya Thevar either, but he is Peri Pandi's favourite protégé. If this alliance helps patch up my relationship with the Maruthu brothers, then I should have my Vellachi married to Vengan.

'Vengan would be a good choice for Vellachi, Peri Pandi. We should go ahead with this alliance.'

A broad smile broke out on the commander's face.

'Thank you, my queen. We should begin preparations for a grand wedding!'

After the court astrologers picked out a suitable date, Vellachi and Vengan Udaya Thevar were married with pomp and grandeur. The simmering rift between Velu Nachiyar and the Maruthu brothers seemed to have healed, if only at a superficial level.

A few months later, Periya Maruthu Pandiyar was with his younger brother in his office in Kalayar Koil, discussing the finances of the army, when some revenue officers arrived.

Addressing the prime minister, one of the officers said, 'We bear catastrophic news, my lord. The ruler of Ramanathapuram has blocked the road between Tirunelveli and Thondi. Due to the blockade, we are not able to collect the custom duty at Parthibanur. Since this is the harvest season, we are losing a significant amount of revenue. We could face a precipitous drop in collection this year, my lord.'

'The Arcot stooge has finally shown his true colours! But why is he taking such drastic actions? What has triggered him?'

'I have been told that the king has taken offence at the rejection of his marriage proposal for Princess Vellachi. To make matters worse, the princess is now married to Prince Vengan Udaya Thevar. Raja Muthuramalinga believes this decision was taken at your behest and this blockade is a retaliation against your actions.'

Periya Maruthu Pandiyar stood up in anger.

'That mongrel! He thinks he can intimidate us! I will teach him a lesson!'

Before he could go any further, Chinna Maruthu Pandiyar calmed him down.

'Now is not the time for open warfare, Peri Pandi. We need to offer a calibrated response. If he thinks he can choke our economy by the blockade, we need to show him that we control the jugular vein of the Ramanathapuram kingdom itself.'

'What do you propose we do, Chinna Pandi?'

'Divert the Vaigai river away from Ramanathapuram. A few weeks of thirst will bring him back to his knees. Order your men to divert the river on a war footing. He should feel the impact before the summer ends.'

The commander ordered his generals to spare no effort, money or men to divert the river away from Ramanathapuram. The river was already running thin in the dry heat of summer and, in the course of the next few weeks, the diversion was complete.

But it did not yield the expected results. Soldiers from Ramanathapuram and Sivaganga engaged in clashes at the border of the two kingdoms. Periya Maruthu Pandiyar didn't take this aggression kindly and ordered his troops to push back the Ramanathapuram soldiers and further enter the kingdom to raze their military posts.

As one action led to another escalated reaction, fears began to mount that this would lead to a full-scale war between the two Marava kingdoms.

The English, who were now playing the role of military enforcers for Arcot in the latter's southern provinces, sought to defuse the tension by initiating diplomatic efforts with the Maruthu brothers, Rani Velu Nachiyar and Muthuramalinga Sethupathi. Colonel Welsh began written correspondence with each of the parties and tried to effect a ceasefire with options for concessions that each party could offer to halt the hostilities.

Velu Nachiyar received a letter at Sivaganga.

The Maruthu brothers are willing to withdraw our troops from Ramanathapuram if I choose Vellachi as my successor. The diverted river will be routed back to Ramanathapuram, and Raja Muthuramalinga will lift the blockade of the road between Tirunelveli and Thondi. If I give acquiescence to this proposal, then the doors for Gowri Vallabha Thevar to become the next ruler of Sivaganga will shut forever. Worse, he may be banished from Sivaganga.

The rani put the letter on the table. Her heart ailment had become worse with the passage of time. Her desire to hand over the kingdom to a capable person was waning.

I need to yield. For the sustenance of peace in the kingdom, I need to give up my desire. My time is near and I can look after my people only for so long. Vellachi has never been a strong girl, both mentally and physically. Her husband Vengan Udaya Thevar will essentially run the kingdom and the boy takes his orders from Peri Pandi, being his protégé. The kingdom will ultimately go into the hands of the Maruthu brothers. They already control the army, administration and treasury of the kingdom. They will now control the throne as well. I have no doubt about the intentions of Peri Pandi and Chinna Pandi. They seek the best for Sivaganga. But their methods will put Sivaganga in harm's way. All I can do is pray that Vellachi and Vengan lead the country forward in the right direction.

Moving to her writing table, she drafted the reply to the English. She would abdicate and hand over the kingdom to her daughter, Vellachi. In return, all she asked for was peace in Sivaganga.

With all parties in agreement, Vellachi took over as the next queen of the Sivaganga and the Maruthu brothers continued in their existing roles. Gowri Vallabha Thevar, fearing for his life, escaped to Arantangi and sought protection under the Tondaimans of Pudukkottai. Peace returned to the kingdom.

Velu Nachiyar called for a meeting with the Maruthu brothers, her daughter and son-in-law.

'My heart ailment has grown worse over the last few years. My doctors have recommended that I proceed to Puducherry and avail myself of the medical facilities of the French. They believe I stand a better chance of recovery there. I have handed over all the responsibilities of the kingdom to you all. I know Sivaganga will be safe in your hands. So, I am heeding my doctors' request and leaving for Puducherry soon.'

A week later, Rani Velu Nachiyar bid goodbye to everyone at Sivaganga and proceeded to Puducherry.

Start of the retreating monsoon of 1793, the Sivaganga palace

It was dusk when Velu Nachiyar disembarked from the palanquin outside the Sivaganga palace. Her hair was frayed and more grey than black. She had aged almost a decade, even though it had been only three years since she had left Sivaganga. Her movements had significantly slowed down. Her eyes were sunken in and red from incessant grief and fatigue. Dried tears streaked her wrinkled face.

'Where are they?' she stuttered.

'The bodies of Rani Vellachi and her infant daughter are in their personal quarters, your highness. Everyone awaits your presence,' the courtier replied.

The queen mother was guided to the personal quarters of Rani Vellachi.

The men, including the Maruthu brothers and Vengan Udaya Thevar, were in the quarters adjacent to hers. The queen's room was filled with the womenfolk of the palace and their muffled sobs.

Velu Nachiyar saw her daughter Vellachi, adorned in a fine silk saree and royal jewellery, lying on a bed, with her infant daughter in a cradle next to her.

'Both the queen and her daughter passed away due to a mysterious illness. Queen Vellachi's chronic poor health only exacerbated the illness. None of the doctors could cure her. She didn't suffer much pain, for both the queen and the princess passed away within a few days after contracting the illness.'

Velu Nachiyar acknowledged the explanation and placed a garland over the corpses of her daughter and granddaughter.

'Let's go ahead with the last rites for my child and grandchild. There's nothing more to be done.'

Following the queen mother's order, preparations for the last rites of the queen and princess of Sivaganga began.

The next night, the Maruthu brothers were having a private dinner in their personal quarters when Chinna Maruthu Pandiyar said, 'These are complicated times, Peri Pandi. We can't keep the throne empty for long. We need to begin preparations for the coronation of Vengan Udaya Thevar and his second wife, your daughter Muthathal, as the queen.'

'Yes, we need to begin in earnest. These are complicated times. We never know what tricks the English have up their sleeve.'

'After signing the Carnatic Treaty with Arcot last year and taking over the revenue administration of Arcot, the English deployed revenue collectors to Tirunelveli and Ramanathapuram and now they are constantly harassing my revenue officers for the long-overdue annual tributes. The English are more persistent than Arcot when it comes to money. They deposed Muthuramalinga Sethupathi from the throne of Ramanathapuram for not paying the annual tribute. They could very well come after us if we let the throne remain empty.'

'The real reason Muthuramalinga Sethupathi was removed was because he supported Veerapandiya Kattabomman, the king of Panchalankuruchi, and his anti-English activities.'

'We support Veerapandiya Kattabomman against the English too!'

'So, we could be next, Peri Pandi. The fool Muthuramalinga Sethupathi was against everybody – the English, Arcot and even us. If only he had sided with us, he would still be sitting on the Ramanathapuram throne. Now that's a lost cause. We need to focus on Sivaganga. We need to fill the throne and safeguard the independence of our kingdom. At the same time, we must discreetly continue our work with Gopal Nayakar and Veerapandiya Kattabomman to take down the English.'

'What are the English up to now, Chinna Pandi?'

'My spies have told me that the English are trying to position Gowri Vallabha Thevar as the next king of Sivaganga. The empty throne has caught their attention.'

'Don't worry, Chinna Pandi, we will soon have Vengan Udaya Thevar on the throne. I will have the astrologers pick a suitable day for his coronation.'

'What about the queen mother? Should we consult her?'

'She hasn't come out of her quarters since performing the last rites of Rani Vellachi. I think she is still in a state of mourning. We can't delay our actions while waiting for her approval. Time is of the essence.'

Rani Velu Nachiyar was alone in her room. She had barely eaten and wasn't taking any appointments. Her heart ailment had progressively worsened since arriving in Sivaganga. She was on heavy medication during her stay in Puducherry. But the news of the deaths of her daughter and granddaughter broke her physically and mentally. Only the punctuality of the French doctors in her entourage ensured that she took her medicines on time.

Her personal courtier entered the room.

'The prime minister and the commander-in-chief have chosen a date for the coronation of Prince Vengan Udaya Thevar as the next king of Sivaganga. They have requested you to preside over the ceremony, queen mother,' he announced.

'Let them go ahead with the coronation. I have nothing to add there. My absence shouldn't be an obstacle,' she said softly.

'Sure, queen mother. Here are some letters from the English

addressed to Queen Vellachi, which she couldn't answer due to her ill health. As the rest are busy with the coronation, would you like to peruse them?'

Velu Nachiyar wasn't interested in the politics of the land anymore, but something told her that she must take the letters.

'Yes. Give them to me,' she stretched out her hand.

Velu Nachiyar's sad face turned to one of concern looking at the volume of letters.

'Please have the Maruthu brothers visit me at the earliest,' she told the coutier.

The next day, the Maruthu brothers arrived in the queen mother's quarters.

'I have been through a few letters from the English demanding the annual tribute,' Velu Nachiyar said. 'We haven't replied to any of them. The tone and intent of the English seem very aggressive. What do you plan to do Chinna Pandi, Peri Pandi?'

The commander replied in an assuring tone, 'There is nothing to worry about, my queen. We are more than capable of defending our Sivaganga and remain stronger than ever. We now have more than 12,000 soldiers right here in Sivaganga and enough capable men stationed in Tirupattur and Kalayar Koil as well. Most of them are trained in the methods of western warfare and they also wield imported arms and ammunition. The English can't do any harm to us. We are secure, my queen.'

'Tipu Sultan of Mysuru just lost a war against the English. They must surely be stronger than before and might exploit this period of calm in the north to attack us. We need a plan of action, Peri Pandi.'

The prime minister was quick to add, 'The defeat of our ally Tipu Sultan is merely an aberration, my queen. He still stands strong. We are the bulwark against the English here in the south. They haven't dared to challenge us here for the past few years.'

'But Chinna Pandi, they are already here in the south. They practically control all Arcot territories. They are allies of Travancore to our west. Their troops and revenue collectors are already present in Tirunelveli and Ramanathapuram. The Pudukkottai Tondaimans are actively collaborating with the English. We are practically surrounded by the English. We are the last of the Marava countries still standing.'

'We are the strongest of the Marava countries. That's the reason we are still standing, queen mother. We are already working on a plan to drive out the English from the Marava lands and are collaborating with Veerapandiya Kattabomman and Gopal Nayakar to attack the weak links of the English. Our troops have tasted success a few times already.'

Periya Maruthu Pandiyar added, 'We will never let down the honour of Sivaganga. You can trust us.'

'I have the utmost faith in you two. But I am worried that we face an uphill battle here.'

'Well, then we'll fight harder, but we won't give up,' Chinna Maruthu Pandiyar replied.

'I have seen other letters, which hint at the English endorsing Gowri Vallabha Thevar as the next king of Sivaganga.'

The Maruthu brothers grimaced in anger.

Periya Maruthu Pandiyar was the first to lose his cool.

'Vengan Udaya Thevar is our king and he will remain so!'

Velu Nachiyar had lost the will to argue with the Maruthu brothers at this juncture.

'I bear no ill will against Vengan Udaya Thevar, Peri Pandi, and I am not against your decision to enthrone him. My only worry is that we are giving the English a reason to act against us. When I took back our home, thirteen years ago, my only wish was for lasting peace. The suffering should have ended when we returned from our exile. But now, we are dangerously close to another war with the English. I don't want my people to suffer the consequences of another war.

'The only people who will suffer now will be the English.'

'I lost everything I loved during our past struggle, but we eventually succeeded. It is our responsibility to protect what we won back that day. All our sacrifices will be in vain if we lose them in another war. I trust you will keep the interests of Sivaganga paramount. I know of your hatred towards the English and Arcot. But our anger should not blind us from our goal, which is to secure Sivaganga's future and lead our people in the right direction.'

Kneeling before Velu Nachiyar and holding her hand, Chinna Maruthu Pandiyar said, 'Our lives have been pledged to the protection of our home. We will spare no effort when it comes to the security and integrity of our kingdom. We will always endeavour to take Sivaganga to greater heights.'

Periya Maruthu Pandiyar too knelt and held Velu Nachiyar's other hand.

'Thank you, Chinna Pandi, Peri Pandi,' she said with a slight nod.

Thanking the queen mother in return, the Maruthu brothers left the quarters. Velu Nachiyar was all alone now.

The tide is turning against us. Everything and every action taken by our adversaries strengthens this feeling in my gut –

I am counting the last days of an independent Sivaganga. It is my misfortune that I have lived for so long to see so many of my loved ones die in front of me. It's my fault for putting my Vellachi in such a perilous situation. My inaction led to the deaths of my daughter and granddaughter. Now, I leave my Sivaganga in a dangerous state of affairs. I doubt if Chinna Pandi and Peri Pandi can gauge the heights of the challenge that will soon be upon us. The worst thing, though, is that I can't do anything to remedy the situation. I am a helpless old woman now. I can't watch Sivaganga die I need to leave.

Velu Nachiyar got into bed and closed her eyes, but she couldn't sleep.

The next morning, she called on the Maruthu brothers again.

'Peri Pandi, Chinna Pandi, my heart ailment grows worse with every passing day. I don't want to be a burden to you or anybody here. I seek to lead the last days of my life in peace and away from Sivaganga. I will take my small entourage and head to Virupatchi. The very place where we first began our retaliation against the English. Please keep Sivaganga and its people safe.'

'I am saddened to see you leave but your health is paramount, queen mother. We wish you a relaxing retired life. Rest assured, the kingdom and its people are in safe hands.'

Saying goodbye, Velu Nachiyar headed out of Sivaganga, one last time.

On reaching the bastion of Gopal Nayakar, she found that the mansion's glory days were long gone but the memories of the place were still fresh in her mind and brought a smile to her face. The yard where she first trained the all-women Udaiyal army was still open. The office of Thandavaraya Pillai was still intact. A few of the progeny of the mandai dogs reared by Periya Maruthu Pandiyar were still loitering around. Remnants of a few valaris forged under the direction of Chinna Maruthu Pandiyar were lying in the now burnt-down barracks. Gopal Nayakar himself had moved out of the mansion and was waging a military struggle against the English. But from here on, this was Velu Nachiyar's home.

Detaching herself entirely from the politics of the land, Velu Nachiyar continued leading a life of retirement. The French doctors who accompanied her tried their best to arrest her deteriorating health but it was a losing battle. Three years later, in 1796, her heart ailment finally got the better of her and the warrior queen of Sivaganga passed away in her sleep.

Epilogue

THE MARUTHU BROTHERS CONTINUED THEIR FIGHT AGAINST the English after the death of Rani Velu Nachiyar. They notched up many successes and freed many of their comrades from English prisons. The English, on their part, were focused on their conflict with Mysuru in the north and so they endured defeats in the south without retaliating against the Maruthu brothers.

Coordinating with Veerapandiya Kattabomman, Gopal Nayakar and other like-minded leaders, the Maruthu brothers scaled up their operations against the English by attacking larger English military outposts. But in 1799, after the death of Tipu Sultan and the defeat of Mysuru, the English concentrated all their efforts and resources in the south. They began diplomatic efforts and public relation campaigns to portray the Maruthu brothers in a bad light amongst the rulers, nobles and common citizenry of the region. Taking it on as a challenge, Chinna Maruthu Pandiyar brought out the now famous Jambu Dweepa Declaration – one of the earliest collective calls for rebellion against the English in the Indian subcontinent, more than half a century before the First War of Independence. The notice was pasted at various temples and forts across south India, calling upon everyone, irrespective of caste, creed or religion, to stand up against the English and defeat them. He specifically called on the seventy-two palegars who ruled over the southern regions of the subcontinent to raise up in arms against their colonizers. The declaration spread across the region like wildfire. Posters of this declaration were posted as far as the Trichy fort in the north. Heeding Chinna Maruthu Pandiyar's call, many joined the effort. This was the start of the Palegar Wars with the English.

In 1799, Veerapandiya Kattabomman was captured and executed by the English, and they went after more of his allies. The Maruthu brothers openly offered refuge to the former's brother, Oomaidurai, in Sivaganga and even accorded a grand welcome to him. This served as the trigger for the English to begin their invasion of Sivaganga.

Slowly but steadily, the English, under the leadership of Colonel Innes, Colonel Macaulay and Lieutenant Colonel Agnew, razed many forts in the kingdom and defeated the Sivaganga army in various battles, finally capturing Sivaganga, Kalayar Koil and other important power centres in the south.

But the Maruthu brothers still wouldn't give up. They retreated deep into the forests and continued guerrilla warfare against the English just as they had under Rani Velu Nachiyar's rule. But it was different this time. The English, hell-bent on eliminating their enemies, brought in reinforcements and waged a continuous war against the Maruthu brothers and their allies. They constantly scoured through the forests, squeezing the Sivaganga leaders out of their hideouts.

The unrelenting pressure from the English finally led to the capture of the Maruthu brothers in 1801. Following their capture, Chinna Maruthu Pandiyar and Periya Maruthu Pandiyar were executed in Tirupattur. Vengan Udaya Thevar was banished from the kingdom and, in his place, Gowri Vallabha Thevar was coronated the king of Sivaganga by the English. But later, under the Permanent Settlement Act, the kingdom of Sivaganga was downgraded to a zamindari system of administration and Gowri Vallabha Thevar became the first zamindar of Sivaganga. As a result, Sivaganga lost the right to raise or maintain a standing army. Its foreign affairs and security came under the direct control of the English. Indigenous weapons such as valaris and marus were banned with immediate effect and revenue collection was taken over by the Company collectors. The conquest of Sivaganga was complete.

By the close of the Palegar Wars, the English had become the masters of southern India.

Author's Note and Acknowledgements

WHILE STUCK IN TRAFFIC ONE DAY, I WAS ASKED BY SOMEONE, 'Tell us a story.' I began the story with the cliché, 'There was this king.' I was stopped right there, 'Why do you always tell stories of kings? Tell us the story of a queen.' It was then that I first narrated the story of Rani Velu Nachiyar. My audience sat captivated as I described the battles in vivid detail, and I saw tears springing to their eyes as I spoke about Kuyili and her sacrifice. I was moved by this display of emotion. Coincidentally, it was around this time that *Hindu BusinessLine* gave me the opportunity to write an article, which I utilized to tell the story of the rani of Sivaganga. After it was published, I thought that was the end of the matter. I received some great feedback from a few people, which I took to be a courtesy. It was also nice to see my article being cited in some journal papers and in a few Wikipedia articles. But the impetus came from a few people with direct interest in Rani Velu Nachiyar, who enquired if I could write a meatier version of the story. Thus began the journey of writing this book.

That's when I discovered there were hardly any primary or secondary sources on the rani. I spent a significant amount of time in southern Tamil Nadu, visiting places, talking to people to know more about the queen, her honourable deeds and the history of Sivaganga. I usually corroborate the stories I hear with written records. But given the dearth of such documentation, I have taken some of the verbal stories at face value and incorporated them into my narrative. So, I might have carried forward the biases that we humans tend to carry in the stories we tell. I have tried my best to stay true to all real events, but certain creative liberties were necessary to form a more cogent narrative.

Field research is hard, and it takes a toll on one's body and mind, especially when searching for stories in the ruins. It was no different for me. The intense heat of the plains of Sivaganga would have broken my spirits if not for the company of my brothers, Gnaneshwar and Tejeshwar, who joined me in my arduous quest to uncover the story of Velu Nachiyar.

My father's encouraging words and my mother's unshakeable faith in me are the bedrock on which this work is built, and they inspire me every day to reach for the skies.

I would like to thank my agent, Anish Chandy, for helping me bring my work to a larger audience. As always, I am grateful for his support.

My good friend, Karan Chawla, who sat through numerous long sessions with me and helped me fine-tune this work. I am deeply indebted to him for his patience.

I would like to thank Teesta Guha Sarkar of Pan Macmillan India for her faith in me and my work. She and her team have again done a tremendous job of polishing my work and holding my hand through my publishing journey. A special shout-out to Shreya Gupta for her meticulous editing and constant feedback that helped me bring out the work in its present form.

My guiding light, my wife Sangeetha, took on a great share of the familial duties even as I immersed myself in this book for prolonged periods of time. I am merely the tip of the iceberg compared to this invisible force that keeps us all afloat. I would like to dedicate this novel to my loving wife.